A Novel

WHO'S THERE?

STEVEN T. THOMAS

Horror Haven Books
3237 Muir Rd.
Dryden, MI 48428
www.authorsteventhomas.com

Printed and bound in the United States of America.

To my wife and kids.

WHO'S THERE?

PROLOGUE

KILLER #1

What's the difference between a serial killer and a politician? The serial killer might listen if you plead with them.

I vividly remember the night I first heard about the Carney family's brutal murder. I was sitting in my living room, sipping on a cup of tea, when the news anchor announced their names with a solemn voice that sent shivers down my spine. It was the first time I had ever heard of the so-called "Knock Knock Killer," and from then on, I became obsessed. The way he executed his kills—no pun intended—was nothing short of brilliant. He would knock on his victim's door, and they would answer it, unsuspecting of the horror that awaited them just beyond the threshold. It was a perfect system—who wouldn't answer their own front door? He was a legend in his own twisted right, and to me, an inspiration.

Fury surged inside me as I watched the story of the Roberts family's senseless murder play out on the news. After years of getting away with near-perfect crimes, he had to come back just because some impudent punk and his foolish companion wanted to uncover his identity? All he would have had to do was stay hidden, ignore it, and yet, he didn't! My entire body shuddered with rage as my fists clenched tightly at the thought of this perpetrator returning.

Cooper and Delilah were foolish and presumptuous to try to uncover Tom's true identity, but I wanted him dead just as much as they did. Still, Tatum was an even bigger fool for loving a murderer and seeing beauty in his cold-blooded crimes. As soon as she was gone, my mission became clear; Cooper Cobb and Delilah Carney must pay for their meddling with an evil that they had no idea existed until it was unleashed upon them. Their destruction will be my legacy, and when they are gone, the chill of death that has been following me will come to pass. They may have thought they uncovered something dark and twisted when they found out who Tom was, but what they really unleashed was me: the darkest embodiment of vengeance and wrath that this world has ever seen.

PART 1

CHAPTER ONE

COOPER COBB
THURSDAY, JUNE 22ND

"Welcome to *True Crime with Cee and Dee*," I say as the recording begins.

Podcasting is in our blood. After we took down the Knock Knock Killer, we decided we would swear off podcasting. The *Knock Knock Podcast* was making us a fortune and it wasn't hard work to do at all. It seemed like a great life, but no one could stay still for long, so we decided to go back to our roots and podcast about True Crime as a whole. We were determined to go back to the early podcasting days of covering just any True Crime story that came across our radar.

We don't do live shows anymore either; we don't need to, and it opened us up to things we don't ever want to invite again. We've been doing great since Tom was stopped and I finally popped the question—we are getting married next year. I couldn't be happier.

I look up and across the table in our new recording studio at Delilah and give her a smile. She smiles back. The love we share is unmatched; it's amazing. If someone would have told me even a year ago that we would be together and planning a wedding, I'd have told them they were insane.

Infinite Podcasting Network, our show's agency, begged us to come back and record some more. We became the number one True Crime podcast across all platforms after we live streamed the Knock Knock Killer's takedown. We made them so much money they gave us an offer we couldn't refuse, plus they paid for us to move and start a new life.

Michigan is a gorgeous place to live if you're in the right area, and that was our one stipulation. We wanted to keep with a more rural environment and we didn't want to move to Detroit, which was the first offer they made to us and we immediately turned it down. They ended up allowing us to choose where we wanted to live and we settled on Lexington. It's a smaller town than Milan, and that's just the way we like it.

The new show doesn't have nearly the amount of listeners that the *Knock Knock Podcast* had, but that's to be expected. The old show had a story and people became heavily invested in it. It was like a favorite book or TV show for some listeners. Such shows are hard to replicate. The topic that we covered was actively happening, and it wasn't until we started digging—I still regret nothing—that the number of listeners truly exploded.

"On today's episode, we are discussing two of America's most notorious killers to have ever existed," I say into the microphone, "Ted Bundy and Charles Manson."

"Did you know that Charles Manson, in an interview, called Bundy a poopbutt?" Delilah asks.

We share a laugh and she pulls the clip up on YouTube to let everyone listen. It's true. He did call Bundy a poopbutt; also a rumpkin and a mama's boy.

What a weird dude.

There is one thing that I regret about the old show and it might seem like I regret ever starting it, but, I think it's one of those things that come with fame. I've had to change my phone number several times since the news broke that we took him down. The pranks accelerated faster than I could have anticipated—tons of fans texting me nonstop pretending to be a copycat killer. One person even went far enough to try to make me believe he was Tom and that we didn't actually kill him. I know that to be false. I slit his throat, I watched as the light left his eyes, and I am the one that ended him once and for all.

We finish up the episode and I signal to our engineer to cut the recording. That's been a weird thing, too. Before, we were on our own, but now, we have a full team. Infinite really outdid themselves with this move.

"Good job, you two," I hear in my headphones.

"Thanks, Remi," I say back.

I walk around the table as Delilah is taking off her headphones and grab her tightly around her waist. She stares into my eyes for a moment and we enjoy the presence of one another. It's our ritual after each episode. We have to remind ourselves that we aren't just partners on the show or roommates anymore.

I'm interrupted by buzzing in my pocket, but I don't want to check it. I don't want to pull my eyes off of her.

"You should probably check that," she says, "it could be Riley."

Riley is flying in tomorrow and staying with us for a couple weeks to help with the wedding planning. I told him he didn't have to do it, but he's my best man *and* my best friend so he feels like it's one of his obligations. Once he gets an idea in his head, he doesn't stop and I don't dare stand in his way.

My hand slowly moves down to my pocket and I feel the familiar weight of my phone. I pull it out, my eyes scanning the unfamiliar number on the screen. I try unsuccessfully to suppress my anxiety, but a feeling of dread seems to be emanating from within as my heart races like a freight train against my ribcage. Delilah stares at me, her expression one of pity mixed with curiosity as she witnesses my fear and confusion.

"What is it?" She asks.

"I…I'm not sure," I say, still staring at the screen.

I turn the phone around and as soon as Delilah sees the text, her face contorts with fear in perfect sync with mine. The room is filled with an oppressive silence for a few moments as we look deep into each other's eyes. Then, like a tsunami, the terror of what we experienced just under a year ago comes crashing over us again. Our insides are boiling with dread and Delilah stumbles to the corner of the room, plunging her head into a nearby trash can and heaving until her stomach is empty. I cringe at the awful sound, but it doesn't erase the terror still filling my gut. She stands up, wiping away her tears and vomit from her lips, holding back sobs as she walks closer to me.

"What does this mean?" she asks.

"I'm not sure," I say, "but it doesn't *feel* like a prank this time."

I can't take my eyes off the phone, transfixed by the message displayed on the screen. I want to believe that this must be some kind of joke, an innocent prank played at my expense. But logic tells me there's something more sinister lurking beneath the words. I'm paralyzed with indecision; I know all too well how quickly this kind of thing can spiral out of control.

Knock Knock, Cooper and Delilah.

I grip my phone and assume the position to type a reply.

"Don't," Delilah says, "don't do it."

"I need to," I say, not looking back up at her as I type.

Who's there?

CHAPTER TWO

COOPER COBB

I can't believe this is happening again. The thought that the killer, or even a copycat, might be back makes my blood run cold. I had assumed that we'd put an end to it all, but clearly we were wrong. All I can think is that our investigation must have stirred up someone's ire and now they are out for revenge. This time around, there are a couple of major issues that make this situation far worse than before. Do we get involved or do we leave it alone? If we take no action, the problem may escalate and catch us off guard. But if we do get involved, more people could die for our troubles. The other problem is that there have been no clues or killings—yet. I had assumed that our efforts had killed any memory of Tom's existence, but evidently it was not enough.

I'm sitting in my office with my face in my palms doing what I do best: stressing. I'm just glad I got to live a little bit of time with low anxiety before this happened. Delilah was already begging me on the way home to leave it alone. I know she doesn't want to live through this again—shit, I don't want to do this again—but I feel like it's my responsibility to take care of the problem. We are the ones that started this and we are the reason that someone else is out there looking for us. In my daze, I hear a light tap on my door.

"Come in," I say.

Delilah opens the door and I turn around and look at her as if I expected someone else. I immediately turn back around because I don't want to give her a reason to talk me out of what I think I've already decided. She walks over and wraps her arms around me from behind, resting her head on my shoulder.

"You okay?" she asks.

"I'm okay," I say, still trying not to look at her.

"I know what we have to do," she says, "but I don't think you're going to like it."

She backs off and unwraps her arms from around my neck as I turn in the office chair and look at her. We stare at one another for a moment and don't speak. She looks embarrassed by whatever she is thinking.

"We," she starts with a slight stutter in her voice, "need to catch this mother fucker. Before he hurts *anyone*."

"Wow," I say.

It's the only word I can manage to get out. I didn't think she would be on board so easily. I thought this was going to take a lot of talking and a ton of negotiation. *This isn't us anymore. We don't do this. The only reason we did last time was because of the show and we owed it to our fans.* I wonder why she's so willing to put both of us in danger.

"Yeah," she says, "we can't let it get out of hand like last time. We need to get ahead of him."

"The only problem is we have nothing. This person, whoever they are, hasn't done anything yet. We have even less to go off of than we did with Tom."

"I know," she says.

"But there's one thing we are good at," I say.

"What's that?"

"We are fantastic at getting a killer to come out of hiding."

She smiles and I smile back.

CHAPTER THREE

DELILAH CARNEY

I had a feeling something was off the second I looked at that text message, and my stomach churned. It was like all the nausea-inducing images I'd seen before—videos of surgery, people vomiting—but worse. All normal triggers for me, yet this felt… different. Even when I was left to discover my own parents and sister dead in the living room of my old home, I hadn't experienced this level of dread.

Taking a deep breath, I set a timer on my phone for two minutes and open Facebook to take my mind off things for a while. But no matter how many articles or memes I scroll through, I couldn't stop thinking about it. My gaze flashes to the counter in the bathroom; nothing revealed yet. Back to the timer—still one minute and forty-five seconds left.

Calm down, Delilah.

I didn't even feel this stressed out when I left Cooper to go to the cops. When he was facing off against Tom. I was worried, sure, but I had my mind set on making sure he was safe and the proper people were there to help him. Turns out he didn't need their help. I am still so proud of him for that.

A minute and thirty seconds remaining.

As I open TikTok, the longest two minutes of my life start to feel like an eternity. Even though I know resetting my algorithm won't erase the memories of us, I still wish it would. Everywhere I go online, there's a reminder of what happened. My heart starts pounding and I can feel the sweat dripping down my forehead as the time ticks closer to zero. My hands begin to shake and I do all that I can to control them. Knowing there's no escape makes me want to scream out in fear. The last fifteen seconds seem like an eternity and when the timer finally winds down, I jump up from the toilet and grab my hair in a makeshift ponytail. The feeling of nausea overwhelms me until finally, something comes up my throat. It takes all of my strength and courage not to give into it.

I heave the contents of my stomach into the toilet with a rush. My head pounds and my vision swims, confusion overwhelming me until I am able to steady myself and focus on my surroundings.

RING. RING. RING.

My phone had fallen onto the ground, and I fumble for it, hitting snooze before collapsing back onto the cold tiles. Reaching up to the countertop, I grab the white stick and close my eyes, taking one last deep breath before slowly opening them again. The pink plus sign in the window stares back at me from the test.

CHAPTER FOUR

COOPER COBB
FRIDAY JUNE 23RD

I awake to the sunrise shining brightly through our bedroom window. I can hear birds chirping outside and the waves crashing against the shore; the world seems to be at peace—though mine isn't. I blink my eyes a few times to adjust to the light, then sit up on the edge of the bed, rubbing my temples with my hands.

I had a rough night of sleep. I was up almost every hour and every time I closed my eyes, I dreamed of Tom. That sinister smile, those devilish looking eyes haunted my nightmares and infiltrated my mind. I thought I was finally past what happened with him, but evidently not with this new person that's out to terrorize us.

I inhale deeply and I can smell the scent of coffee and bacon filling the air. I hadn't thought to look over and see if Delilah is still in bed, but the scent taking over my nose tells me she's downstairs making breakfast. She's incredible.

I stand up and walk into the bathroom. I look at myself in the mirror and take another deep breath. I grab a Dixie cup from the side of the sink and fill it with water, then open the medicine cabinet, take out a bottle of Xanax, grab a pill, and throw it in my mouth—my one crutch since everything went down.

As I swallow the rest of the water, I can hear quick footsteps running up the stairs. I toss the cup into the garbage can and look over as I hear the bedroom door swing open and Delilah, breathing heavily, enters the room. She is bent down trying to catch her breath and I walk over to her and put my hands on her hips. She looks up at me.

"You…need…to…come…see…this," she gets out between breaths.

We walk downstairs into the living room and she forces me to sit down on the couch. Still out of breath and unable to get a word in, she raises her arm and points to the TV.

"Police have no leads and are asking the public, if they have information, to come forward," the news anchor says.

"What—" I start to say, but Delilah butts in.

"Just…watch," she says.

Just then a banner scrolls across the bottom of the screen and the first couple of words that pop up tell me almost everything I need to know.

```
QUINTUPLE HOMICIDE IN LEXINGTON. WHOLE
FAMILY DEAD. POLICE HAVE NO LEADS. CALL LPD
IF YOU HAVE INFORMATION.
```

I sit and stare in awe with my mouth hanging open. I can feel Delilah's stare piercing into the side of my head, but I can't manage to turn and look at her.

"He's back," I say, still looking forward.

"He's back," she says.

He can't be back. I killed him. Yet, this undeniable feeling of déjà vu has been clawing at my very soul like an ancient beast. Even though it's only one family murdered, a sickening dread washes over me that this is far from the last. But I remain hopeful that I am wrong and all of this is just an isolated incident. Then again, the timing is too eerily perfect. A mysterious text dropped into my phone yesterday and today death arrives in our city—I refuse to believe this could be merely coincidence.

The two of us continue to stare at the TV expectantly as if they are going to magically receive some new information. We watch as they show shot after shot of the outside of the house where the crime took place, and we see a reporter trying to get closer to the home being stopped by a police officer who throws his hand over the camera lens.

"Should," I begin to say, "I go to the police and let them know about the text?"

"We know how that worked out before, Cee," she says.

"So, we are on our own again?" I ask.

"We are on our own," she says.

I glance over and look at the clock on the wall. 8:53 a.m. Riley's flight should be arriving around eleven. He's going to be furious when he finds out and there's no way for us to hide it from him if he's staying with us, but we are going to need all the help we can get.

CHAPTER FIVE

RILEY STEVENS

Thank God, I think as the landing gear touches solid ground again.

I hate flying so much, but it's worth it when I get to come see my best friend. I can't believe they moved, but I definitely understand the motivation. Cooper was messed up after everything happened. Anxiety, panic attacks, depression, the whole event set him off mentally. I get why they wanted to get out of Ohio. New place, new start, new life and if I could have, I would have gone with them.

I pull my phone out of my pocket and turn it back on. As the Apple logo flashes on the screen, the airplane jolts and bounces off the runway and my phone goes flying out of my hand into the aisle. I reach over, attempting to catch it, but all I end up doing is hitting it even further out of reach and it lands in the lap of another passenger across from me.

I can feel the redness and heat of embarrassment flash across my face, but the gentleman who caught it just laughs at me and hands it back.

"Sorry," I say.

"It's okay, man," he says.

I look at the time: 11 a.m. We are right on schedule, thankfully. I can't wait to get off this plane. I pull up the messages app, click Cooper's name, and type a message letting him know I've landed and I'll see him soon. I lock my phone screen and almost immediately, the device vibrates in my hand as a text message comes through. The contact reads "Unknown" and I swipe to open the message.

`Knock Knock, Riley. See you soon.`

I gulp as I digest the message on screen. No way, it has to be a prank. Cooper has to be messing with me. He wouldn't, would he? He knows I was already anxious to make this trip and with how messed up he's been, I don't think he would try to pull something like that on me. I consider texting back, but think better of it when another message comes through.

`I can't wait to slice Cooper up in front of you.`

Do I tell Coop, or keep this from him?

CHAPTER SIX

COOPER COBB

Driving to the airport felt like one of the most grueling trips of my life. As we sit at the airport waiting for Riley, an internal battle is raging in my head. I'm not too sure I should say anything, and Delilah hasn't been much help in the decision-making either. I tried asking her about it, but she seems to be deep within her own thoughts and I'm trying to give her a little space. I don't want her to think my obsession is going to come back. We *do* need to talk about this, though.

"Dee," I say with a little hesitation in my voice, "I need your opinion. Do I tell Riley or not?"

"I don't know, Cooper," she says, "on one hand, it might be a good idea, but on the other, I just don't know."

Riley wasn't on board with us even pursuing the Knock Knock Killer to begin with, but like a good friend, he was right there when I needed him the most and I'm thankful for him every day. Even though I'm struggling to find the answer, I think I know what I have to do.

I look toward the doors,see him walking outside, and I throw open the door on Delilah's pink Volkswagen. I've attempted talking her into trading it in for something a little less girly, but I've lost that battle—she loves this car and what it now represents for us. I get out and walk up to him, holding a hand out for a handshake and he pulls me in for a bro-hug.

"Riley," I say, "so nice to see you."

"Nice to see you, too, Coop," he says.

"Let me help you with those," I say, as I gesture to his bags.

I grab the bags from him, even though he resists the offer, and I throw them in the trunk. He and Delilah are hugging now and it makes me even more grateful that I have a friend that approves of her and her of him—life is mostly good. The two of them get in the car and, for a moment, I look up as the rumble of jet engines fills the air and a Boeing 747 flies overhead as it takes off.

I get in the car and, almost as if we planned it, I look at Riley and at the same time, the two of us say, "I need to tell you something."

The atmosphere inside the vehicle becomes tense almost immediately and out of the corner of my eye, I can see Delilah's eyes darting back and forth between us. Although the environment is stressful, we share a chuckle because of our synchronicity.

"You first," I say.

Riley digs into his pocket and pulls out his phone, unlocks it, and hands it to me. I read the texts, then turn the phone so Delilah can read them as well. Her eyes begin to well up with tears and I put my hand on her thigh and squeeze slightly in an effort to comfort her. I look up at Riley, he has his head down as if he's ashamed. I pull my phone out of my pocket and hand it to him. He reads for a moment, then looks up at me fearfully.

"What do we do?" He asks.

I glance over at Delilah for a moment and she nods at me in a vote of confidence. I look back up at Riley with a serious look on my face. For the next two weeks, I'm sure there will be no wedding planning. We have a killer to hunt down.

"We fight," I say, confidently.

"We fight," I say, confidently.

CHAPTER SEVEN

COOPER COBB

As we pull into our subdivision, I observe the families out barbecuing and kids playing in their yards. I can't help but feel responsible for what may happen to them in the coming days or weeks. I stare out the window, watch, and almost feel creepy. My brain is blocking almost all sound out. Though I can hear Riley and Delilah talking, in my ears, it's mumbled.

We hit the bump as we pull into the driveway and I come back to reality with a jolt. I look up as though I don't know we are back at our house and Delilah looks at me, concerned. I turn around and Riley is looking at me the same way. I know they're both wondering what my next move is going to be.

Why do I always have to be the point person? I think.

"What?" I ask, acting like I don't know why they are staring.

"Are you okay?" Riley asks.

"Yeah, I'm fine."

I'm not fine.

"Liar," Delilah says with a slight smirk.

"I'm fine, I'm just thinking," I say.

"About?"

"Where to start."

I know where to start and I know what worked the last time. I'm going to have to call him, or her, out. I'm going to have to be blunt because we have nothing to start with this time around. I can't let it get as out of control as last time. We've already had five deaths and we haven't even begun to unravel the mystery now.

I look back out the window and admire the sky. We've been gone most of the day and the sun is beginning to set and is painting the horizon with pinks and oranges as it drops behind the houses on our street. I can't remember the last time I truly just enjoyed the beauty of nature—it's peaceful. The atmosphere inside the car is becoming more tense by the second and I can feel both of them staring at me. I hate feeling like I'm being watched. Delilah breaks the silence.

"At least we know the rules," she says.

I look at her with a confused look on my face and she continues to stare at me with that smirk she gives when she's about to make a smartass comment.

"The rules?" I ask as I turn and look at Riley and he shrugs.

"Yeah, the rules to surviving a horror movie sequel," she says.

Ah, a Scream *reference,* I think. I know it makes her happy so I let her continue.

"The amount of murders is always a lot bigger and the kills are always bloodier and more intense," she confirms.

I knew that's what she was going to say, but hearing her say it out loud was worse than thinking it myself. Just eight months ago back in Ohio, the Knock Knock Killer murdered a total of twenty-six people. How do you top twenty-six killings? That's on par with Gacy. If she's correct, if real life follows the rules of a horror movie, we need to stop this and we need to do it now. The question is: how? How do you hunt a ghost? I make the decision I know I need to.

I reach into my pocket and pull out my phone, then glance at Delilah who suddenly has a worried look in her eyes. I can feel the back of my seat being pulled as Riley leans forward over my shoulder trying to see what I'm doing. I pull up my messages app, then stop for a moment and watch the cursor blink at me, waiting for a reply to be entered, then, I begin to type.

If you want to kill me, come and get me.

I realize that my reply text has a blue background, which means the killer is using an iPhone—not typical for someone using a burner phone. I don't know what it means or if it's a clue or even a way to go, but we have that detail now.

I look back up at Delilah and she has a horrified look on her face, then over to Riley who matches her expression. The vehicle is completely silent until I decide to speak up.

"I'm not doing this shit again," I say.

My phone begins to vibrate, but this time it's the phone call vibration, not a text and the contact name reads "Unknown."

"Don't answer it," Delilah pleads.

But I tap the green answer button and bring the phone to my ear.

"What?" I say forcefully.

"In due time," the voice says on the other end of the line followed by the triple beep of an iPhone call disconnecting.

CHAPTER EIGHT

COOPER COBB

"What do we know?" I ask Delilah and Riley.

They're staring at me like I'm crazy as I feverishly pull out everything we have on the original Knock Knock Killer. If this person is following in his footsteps, chances are there is going to be a pattern we need to follow—or so I think.

"Nothing," Delilah says, "we know nothing."

"Has the news mentioned a murder weapon?" I ask.

"No, not yet," Delilah says.

I look over and observe her. Her face looks as white as a ghost and she has dark circles around her eyes. She looks almost sick and she is swaying slightly as she stands in the corner of the room. I notice she's kind of staring at me, maybe more so through me. She's looking in my direction, but doesn't seem like she's truly looking *at me*.

"Are you okay?" I ask.

"Yeah I'm—" she starts, then stops and throws a hand over her mouth and runs out of the room.

I look at Riley sitting in the office chair at my desk where he is scouring social media and news sites for information. We make eye contact and he can see I'm asking him, without asking verbally, what that was all about and he shrugs his shoulders.

Delilah comes back promptly, breathing a little heavier than normal, but doesn't acknowledge what just happened and I decide to ignore it as well.

Maybe she ate something that didn't agree with her, I think.

I'm pulling the last of the files out of the Bankers Box and tossing them to the floor. The carpet is littered with paper and manila folders, all with information that I saved from after we beat Tom at his sick, twisted game.

"We need to know what he—" I start, but Riley cuts me off.

"Two weapons," he says. I look up at him.

"Excuse me?" I ask.

"Breaking news—whoever this is used two weapons. Each of the victims were found with stab wounds *and* a single gunshot to the head," he says.

"The kills are always much more elaborate," Delilah says.

"That's not elaborate, that's just sadistic," I say.

"I think the word you're looking for is thorough," Riley says.

I give Riley a look of disapproval, then move my eyes to Delilah who is snickering in the corner of the room at the comment. I give her a small smirk and admire her for a moment. I'm so happy she's decided to marry me and I wish we could just focus on that, though I think she understands. I'm a little worried that something will happen this time and one of us won't be around anymore. I shake my head and kick the thought out of my mind.

We've beat it once, we can do it again, I think.

Delilah reaches down into her pocket, pulls out her phone, and stares at it for a moment, then looks at me with fear in her eyes. I can see her hands begin to shake and her face becomes flush.

"What is it?" I ask.

Riley looks up and stares blankly, silently. Delilah walks over to me and turns her phone around to show me a text message that she's just received.

`Knock Knock from Milan, Delilah.`

The three of us look back and forth, myself looking at Delilah, then to Riley, then back to Delilah. It's an unspoken agreement that we have no idea what to do, but that we need to take action and we need to do it quickly. Suddenly, all three of our phones begin to ding and vibrate at the same time. Delilah turns her phone back around to look at it while Riley and I dig ours out of our pocket.

It's a group text message to all three of us from a restricted phone number and simultaneously the three of us unlock our phones to read it.

`Start planning your funerals.`

CHAPTER NINE

RILEY STEVENS

Lexington feels so different from Milan—makes no sense. The small town feel is there just like it, but smaller. Laying in bed in the dark, I'm staring at the ceiling enjoying the peaceful sounds of Lake Huron lapping against the shore. Even at night, I can hear seagulls squawking as they fly through the air and the distant sound of tires against pavement.

I can't believe it. Is this really happening again? I think to myself.

Though I feel at peace right now, I'm not. My mind is racing about who is doing this again and why. What are their motivations? So many questions and no answers. I fought Cooper and Delilah last time—I distanced myself. I knew Cooper would get himself into some shit and I didn't want any part of it. Now I have no choice; I'm stuck here. If I had actually helped them solve it the last time, I wouldn't be so in the dark right now.

I don't know how they do it. They act so calm, cool, and collected. When they received those text messages, they barely flinched. They're used to it. They shouldn't have to be, but it hasn't been very long since those messages stopped coming through. The thoughts and memories are still very much fresh in their brains.

I'm tossing and turning; I can't seem to shut my brain off long enough to close my eyes and fall asleep. I reach over to the bedside table and grab my phone to check the time. 2:13 a.m. I open Facebook and start scrolling meaninglessly through my news feed. I swipe past memes and other shitposting that litters the platform until I see her name pop up. I stop and click on her profile.

Alicia. She's beautiful with her gorgeous, bright blue eyes, her long brunette hair, her perfect lips. How I landed her is beyond me, but the last two months with her have been incredible. She's caring, understanding, and fun to be around. I haven't told Cooper and Delilah about her yet and haven't really had a moment to think about it since I landed. I was trying to get her to fly out here with me to meet them, but she had other obligations.

My phone begins to vibrate in my hand and the unexpected notification makes me jump. I look away out of panic, afraid to see what may be popping up on the screen. Is it the killer? Is it my mom for some reason? Finally I look down to see a text from Alicia.

You up?

CHAPTER TEN

COOPER COBB
SATURDAY, JUNE 24TH

Sitting on a barstool at the kitchen island is one of my favorite Saturday morning things to do. Delilah is cooking breakfast and I am enjoying a cup of coffee while I watch the news. Riley isn't up yet, so we get to have some alone time before he emerges from his slumber. I love watching her cook and, even though it doesn't feel like the murders will ever be over, at this moment, I can't wait until these moments become Saturday morning cartoons and the pitter patter of tiny feet running across the hardwood floor.

I take a sip of my coffee and Delilah turns around and catches my eye as I admire her beauty. She giggles a little bit then walks up to the island, leaning down on her elbows and staring me in the eyes as she leans forward for a kiss. I meet her halfway and just as our lips touch, the musical jingle for breaking news fills the room from the TV. It startles us and we look up and stare at the screen.

Old habits die hard, I think.

"We have breaking news out of Milan, Ohio this morning where police are on the scene of a grizzly murder," the news anchor announces.

My hands begin to shake and my palms start to get sweaty. Delilah and I look at one another as our hometown is being featured on the national news.

"This devastating news comes mere months after the rural town was rocked by a series of murders that ended with the unmasking of the killer by Milan's own Cooper Cobb and Delilah Carney," she continues.

It's been a while since we heard our names in the news, but this time, we are being called heroes and not being blamed for the murders. It's a nice change of pace. Movement catches my eye in the hallway and I turn my head briefly to see Riley walking out to the kitchen rubbing his eyes and yawning.

"What'd I miss?" he asks, sleepily.

I point at the TV and he looks over, still rubbing his eyes, then they grow wide as he reads the headline at the bottom of the screen:

Murder In Milan. Family Of Three Dead.

"What the hell?" he yells as he turns on his heels and runs back to the guest bedroom.

Delilah and I look at each other; she raises an eyebrow and I shrug, then we turn our attention back to the screen. They've cut from the studio to a wide shot of the home surrounded by caution tape. I can see at least ten police officers walking in and out of the house, but one specific man catches my eye. He's a tall, heavy man and he is wearing a suit.

"Is that Detective Prescott?" I ask.

Delilah leans forward a little bit and squints her eyes, trying to get a better look.

"It is," she says.

I liked Prescott a lot more than I liked Carpenter, that's for sure. They were the two that were assigned to the Knock Knock Killer case eight months ago and the ones that questioned us when we were briefly arrested. I wonder where his partner is?

Riley re-enters the room feverishly typing on his phone. I wonder what's got him all freaked out. Just then, there is a heavy rap on the front door and all of us turn our attention to the door. We've been down this road before and Delilah and I glance at one another. I think we both have an idea of who may be at the door, though we say nothing. I stand up and walk over to the door with my coffee cup still in hand, grab the handle, and open it. A tall, bulky man is standing at the door looking down to me with a stern look on his face.

"Cooper Cobb," he says, "long time no see."

"Hello, Detective Carpenter, what are you doing in Lexington?" I ask, puzzled.

He reaches his hand into the pocket on the inner lining of his jacket and flashes a badge at me showing the Lexington Police Department logo on it.

Why is he working in Lexington now? Did he follow us? I think.

I open the door a little wider so Riley and Delilah can see who I'm talking to. The detective leans to his left to get a better look inside our home and spots Delilah standing in the kitchen with a spatula still in her hand, holding it up as if she is about to smack someone with it.

"Miss Carney," he says.

"Detective," she says, the sound of confusion in her voice.

"May I come in? I just want to ask you two a few questions."

I look at Carpenter, then back to Delilah, then to Riley, then back to the detective. Still gripping my coffee mug by the handle, I look down into the black liquid and hold it up as if I'm about to participate in a toast.

"Coffee?" I ask.

"Just like old times," he says, as he steps through the doorway.

CHAPTER ELEVEN

COOPER COBB

"I'm assuming we aren't under arrest this time," I say with a sarcastic tone as I pour Detective Carpenter a mug of coffee.

He laughs. "No, you're not under arrest this time," he says.

I make my way across the kitchen and set the coffee in front of him. The steam billows from the top of the cup and he grabs it, brings it to his lips, and takes a sip. He looks up at me—I must look a little suspicious right now because I'm staring at him as if I poisoned the drink and am waiting for him to keel over.

"You remembered," he says, "two sugars."

"So, how can we be of assistance to you?" I ask as I back away and lean against the counter.

He continues to sip his coffee and we stay silent. This isn't a side of him I've seen before. Usually he's direct and to the point. Today, he looks like he came over just to hang out as if we've been friends for years. I think it's because we came to an understanding, albeit a silent one, but an understanding nonetheless. I have a feeling he is going to ask me to stay out of things this time, but I won't. I *can't. We* can't

"Well, clearly you've seen the news," he says, gesturing to the TV. I'm just now realizing the volume is still blasting and I reach for the remote and hit the mute button.

"Yes," I say.

"I talked to Detective Prescott this morning and it seems we might have a copycat on our hands. We can't say anything solid yet, but, based on the attack in Milan last night and the attack here in Lexington a couple of days ago, we are being led to believe that is the case," he says.

He lifts his coffee back to his mouth and takes another sip. My eyes dart over his shoulder at Riley who is standing awkwardly about ten feet away from him. I forgot Riley wasn't involved the last time; he didn't want to be. The nonchalance in which I willingly let a detective into our home took him off guard, I'm guessing.

"I guessed that two days ago when the first attack happened here," I say.

"How?" he asks.

"Just a hunch—we've done this dance before," I say, confidently.

"Right," he says, "which is part of the reason I'm here."

I stiffen my posture, preparing for a showdown. I set down my coffee mug onto the counter a little harder than I meant to, the hot liquid spilling over the edge. My chest rises and falls rapidly as I size up Detective Carpenter, almost as if silently challenging him to a duel. I feel Delilah move closer and she takes my hand in hers like an anchor keeping me from lashing out.

"I can't have you two meddling this time," he says, "it worked out before, but there is no guarantee it will work out this time."

Delilah and I had single-handedly solved the case last time with absolutely no help from the local police department. My blood begins to boil. *How dare he?* I think angrily. We could do ten times more than the entire station, whether it's here or in Milan.

"It was great seeing you, Detective," I say, waving my hand toward the door, ushering him out.

He slumps his shoulders, his head hanging heavy. He leans on the island, slowly rises, and turns to meet Riley's gaze. As he sees the fear in Riley's eyes, Detective Carpenter extends his arm towards him for a handshake, but his tone is void of hope as he does so.

"Detective Carpenter," he says.

"R-Riley Stevens," he says, holding his hand out.

"Nice to meet you," Carpenter says.

I stalk behind the detective, my presence looming like a shadow. He suddenly halts in his tracks and spins around to face me, his eyes like daggers ready to be thrown.

"Seriously, Cooper," he says, "if we have a serial killer operating in multiple states, I don't want you to get hurt and I'm sure you don't want Delilah or Riley to get hurt, either. I'll be watching you. Please don't get involved."

I'm holding on to the door and scoff at his bleak attempt at being intimidating because he doesn't scare me anymore. I view him as a big teddy bear these days, especially after the heartfelt voicemail he left me. I don't have it in me to be afraid of him. He keeps his eyes locked on me as he steps down the couple of stairs to the sidewalk in front of our home.

"You know I can't promise that," I say as I slam the door in his face.

I slowly turn, my gaze frozen on Delilah and Riley. The air thickens as we stand in tense silence for an eternity. With one glance, Delilah conveys her message of acceptance to me. Her lips barely upturn into a faint smile of approval as I prepare for the task ahead, knowing that Riley will be unable to stop me.

"Let's get to work," I say with confidence in my voice.

CHAPTER TWELVE

LEXINGTON, MI
KILLER #1

I snatch up the phone with a trembling hand, my thumb hovering over the contact I need. Sweat beads across my forehead as I hit the call button and listen to it ring and ring and ring; each unanswered buzz like a gunshot in my ear. I fumble for the screen and dial her again, but she doesn't answer. A scream builds within me, clawing its way up my throat until I can barely contain it. With a shaking hand, I type out a text message filled with rage and desperation, hitting send before I can reconsider.

My eyes flicker to the TV where breaking news out of Milan flashes on the screen, igniting a proud smile that twists my features into something grotesque. I reach for my pack of Davidoff Primero cigars, fingers fumbling to grab one. It's not particularly expensive, but it's good enough to celebrate what's coming. The first puff tastes sour in my mouth as I ignite it with a flick of my lighter, each puff carrying the weight of anticipation. My gaze drifts to the second phone lying innocently on the table, taunting me with its silence. I pick it up, feeling tears gather at the corners of my eyes as I stare at her photograph—an image that's become both my salvation and damnation. The subtle tear turns into a full-blown cry as I brush it away with trembling fingers.

"Fuck you, Cooper Cobb," I say out loud, "and fuck you, too, Delilah Carney."

I set the phone down and just as it hits the table, it begins to ring. I look over and see it's *her* calling me back. I quickly grab it and press the green button to answer the call.

"Well, hello," I say as if I wasn't expecting her call.

"Hi," she says.

"Are you safe?"

"Yes."

"You did a good job, sweetie. I'm proud of you."

"Thank you."

"Now, let's lure him back to Milan."

CHAPTER THIRTEEN

COOPER COBB

See you in Milan.

The text came through right after Detective Carpenter left the house. It's as if whoever this is is watching us. He—or she—knows what's going on here. I slowly walk to the curtains hanging at the front windows and watch the detective leave the driveway. I debate running out and showing him the text, but this is the same guy that ignored most everything last time. I turn around and look back to Riley and Delilah.

"Another text," I say.

"What's it say?" Delilah asks.

I show it to her and she suddenly looks horrified—I'm more confused than anything. We haven't discussed going back to Milan so why does this person think we will be there? Delilah throws her hands over her mouth and runs out of the room, slamming the bathroom door behind her. I can hear the muffled retching followed by Riley laughing.

"Does she do that a lot?" he asks.

"Just recently," I say, giving him a concerned look.

"Dude, she's totally pregnant," he says, laughing even more now.

"She is *not*," I bark, a little more forcefully than I intended.

Though I don't believe it, his comment puts me in my own head and I think about it for a moment. *What if she is?* There's no one I'd rather start a family with than her, but now that we are chasing down another murderer, or two, that puts her more at risk and I have to do anything I can to protect her. I have to ensure that this ends for good this time—even if I have to lay down my own life to spare hers.

For now I'll leave the idea alone, and if she is, she can come to me and we will handle it when we need to. I know that if I know that to be the truth, it will do nothing but distract me from the task at hand. If she is, I can't raise a kid in a world where the Knock Knock Killer exists—Tom Langford or not.

Delilah walks out of the bathroom and looks at us as if she didn't just empty the contents of her stomach into the toilet. She walks up to me and puts her arms around my neck and stares into my eyes lovingly. She doesn't speak, she just stares at me. I wrap my arms around her midsection and do the same back. I can feel awkwardness radiating off of Riley behind us and Delilah looks over my shoulder at him.

"Care to join?" she asks him sarcastically.

"Get a room," he replies with a laugh.

Delilah looks back to me and nothing in my life has ever felt as perfect as it does when I am with her. I can't believe it took me so long to realize I didn't just love her, but that I was *in love* with her.

"So, what do we do now?" she asks.

I'm always the guy with an answer. I am always the one she looks to for ideas, and right now, I'm stumped. We are in a new town, we don't know anyone, and it's not just one city where the murders are taking place this time around, it's two. We can't split up, we have safety and strength in numbers, but I get the feeling whoever this is is trying to pull us back to our old stomping grounds: the small town of Milan, Ohio—where Riley just flew in from. What would happen if we stayed in Lexington? Would we be able to force them to come to us? If they're anything like Tom, they won't stop. They'll keep killing until they get to us. The warnings will keep coming and they'll compound and get worse and worse.

"I…I don't know," I say, "for once, I'm totally stumped."

The body count is always bigger, I think.

I let go of Delilah and begin pacing in the kitchen, thinking and thinking. Trying to come up with a plan. We have much less to go off of this time around than we did last time, and that's not saying much considering how little we had to work with the last time. Tom, however, didn't care. He wanted us to catch him and he ended up coming to us—my parents almost died because of us, but ultimately made a sacrifice that led to his death.

"Who wants coffee?" I say.

CHAPTER FOURTEEN

COOPER COBB

Standing at the counter at Lexington Coffee Co., my head is spinning, both figuratively and literally. I reach down and grab the counter so I don't fall to the ground and close my eyes. I feel a hand touch my shoulder almost immediately and I open them again to see Delilah worriedly staring at me.

"You okay?" she asks.

"I'm fine," I say reassuringly, "I just got dizzy."

She moves her hand from my shoulder to my midsection to help me stay stable. The barista hands us our coffees and we move to a table and sit down. I take the lid off my coffee and become entranced by the steam wafting out the top of the cup. The sound of chatter seems to dissipate as quickly as the mist does from the heat of the drink and it's almost as if I've lost my sense of hearing.

As quickly as the restaurant became muted, a new voice enters my mind and I can hear it echoing through my ears. The voice is haunting, sinister and distorted, but I can place it easily. I don't think I will ever forget that voice.

"Knock Knock, Cooper Cobb," it says, followed by "did your parents ever tell you that you have a brother?"

I am completely zoned into the imaginary conversation I'm having with Tom Langford and it feels like I'm reliving that night all over again. I think it's time I go talk with a therapist. I try not to share it with Delilah, but I think I might be suffering from PTSD from the ordeal, though, I'm the man, I'm the provider and protector—I need to stay strong.

"You are no brother of mine," I hear as my own distorted voice echoes in my head.

"Cooper, Cooper, Cooper," my own name echoes, then becomes clearer as the world around me comes back into my consciousness.

"Cooper," Delilah says.

I shake the thoughts off and look up. Riley and Delilah are both staring at me wide eyed. I look back and forth between them and they don't say a word.

"Sorry," I say, "thinking."

"Thinking hard," says Delilah, "we've been trying to get your attention for a couple of minutes."

I pick up my mug, clasping it with both hands as the steam rises into my face. The rich aroma of freshly roasted coffee beans wafts through the air and fills my lungs, igniting a fire in my belly. As I take a sip, the scorching liquid glides down my throat, sending shivers throughout my body. I set the cup back down on the saucer and breathe in deeply, feeling renewed and ready for whatever challenges lay ahead.

"What are we going to do?" Delilah asks.

"I have one idea," I say, "but you're not going to like it."

I direct my attention to Riley. "You're *really* not going to like it.

"One thing has become clear, there's two of them again and they're trying to lure us back to Milan. We can't let that happen. They want us in their domain, their comfort zone. We need to retain control. We need to get both of them to come here where *we* keep control."

The oppressive silence between us grows thicker and our three sets of eyes lock in a seemingly never-ending gaze. This feeling of dread is familiar, but there is something new here. In the past two days, eight bodies have been added to the Knock Knock Killer's tally. These two are proving to be far more vicious and tenacious than the killer we had encountered before. I forcefully swallow the last remnants of my coffee, desperately trying to keep my composure.

"The question is, how do we do that?" I ask.

"What if—" Delilah starts, "what if we simply tell them no? We let them know we can't be pushed around or taunted to come back. If they want to kill us, they have to come to Lexington and leave it at that. It might piss them off enough to derail their plan. It worked with Tom when you pushed back."

"That's true, it did work," I say, "but one thing the three of us—sorry you're involved, Riley—have to agree on right here and right now. We stick together. We don't get to split up and send one or two to Milan and leave one or two of us here. No one fights alone. Is that understood?"

"Understood," Delilah and Riley say at the same time.

I breathe a sigh of relief, especially for Riley. I know he likes to go rogue. He showed me that when he ran out of the darkness and tackled Tom to the ground.

My phone begins to ring and we all look over at it with fear on our faces. It shows that it's an unknown number calling in— again. I glance up and look at both of them.

"Don't answer it," Riley says with his voice shaking.

"You have to," Delilah says, "you know you do."

I pick up the phone and pause for a moment, then, "Hello?"

"Hi, Cooper Cobb?" A voice I've never heard before comes through the other end of the phone and I breathe a sigh of relief that it's not the killer. It's a deep man's voice and he almost sounds like Sam Elliot.

"Yeah, this is him." I say, nervously.

"Hi, this is Special Agent Reed Jacobs with the Detroit FBI. I'm calling regarding a recent string of killings between both Michigan and Ohio. I was referred to you by a Detective Carpenter. Is now a good time?" he says.

"There's never a good time anymore," I say jokingly.

He laughs, "Well, I was referred to you because you may have information on this new round of murders—"

"I don't," I say, cutting him off.

"Well, I know you were involved with a Tom Langford who killed multiple people over four years in Milan, Ohio and you were able to take him down. The FBI is requesting your help."

"How much will the FBI be able to do? Milan police couldn't do anything, that's why I got involved," I say.

"We have more resources than them. We are confident we can find the person or persons responsible," he says.

"Persons," I say accusingly.

"You know that to be a fact?" he asks.

"I don't, but deductive reasoning tells me multiple people are operating between the two states."

"Hmm," he says, "good catch. Would you be able to make time to meet with me at the office tomorrow, say, 1 p.m.?"

I look at Delilah and Riley who are intently staring at me. I almost forgot they were sitting there because of the shock of the FBI reaching out to me. They're waiting for me to say something as they have no idea what's being talked about.

"No, I can't," I say to him, an arrogant tone returning to my voice—a tone that I haven't used in a few months.

"And why is that, Mr. Cobb?"

"Because you all gave up last time," I say, "and I don't have any information I haven't already given you. Why would I waste my time?"

"You'd be doing your duty to your hometown, and your country," he says.

"The only duty I have to this country is to pay taxes and die," I say, "nothing more, nothing less."

"Mr. Cobb," he starts, "I'm going to urge you to come meet with me tomorrow. If you don't, you become a person of interest."

"I won't be as soon as I solve this *again* while the FBI and the police give up."

I hang up the phone and Delilah and Riley are still staring into my soul. I look up from the screen and to them as they wait with baited breath for me to tell them what just happened, though I think they can deduce that it wasn't a pleasant phone call.

"The FBI wants us to meet with them," I say, "not a chance. *We* will solve this. Again."

Their mouths fall open.

CHAPTER FIFTEEN

COOPER COBB
SUNDAY, JUNE 25TH

We awoke this morning to news of more murders—this time one in Milan and one in Lexington. A family of four and a single mom with one kid. That's fourteen people dead in the last couple of days. People who didn't have to die. People who died because of us. I try not to let those thoughts infiltrate my head. I know it's not our fault because we can't control other people's thoughts and actions, but our actions, in a roundabout way, caused this. In a way, I caused Tom's murderous rampage.

Stop, Cooper, I think.

The news coverage rolls over and over again and cuts back and forth from Michigan to Ohio as the predators at the news channels catch wind that the FBI is involved in the case now. I consider shutting it off to try to shut my brain off, but I can't. I need to know what's happening and I need to know, if they ever announce it, *how* these people were killed. I need to know what we are up against.

I look away for a moment and down to my phone. I woke up to multiple text messages, emails, and social media notifications. Many of the notifications from our fan pages are listeners begging us to bring back the *Knock Knock Podcast* to solve this new string of murders. The live video of me hunting down and killing Tom became an instant viral hit and it seems our supporters want more.

The emails are the same, except for one that stands out to me. It's from our manager Paul at Infinite Podcasting. He was bombarded with emails from fans just like we were begging him to let us start it up again and I'm surprised by what he sent me.

Cooper,

I've received multiple emails from your listeners regarding the *Knock Knock Podcast* in light of the murders taking place in Lexington and Milan. I have to agree with them. It was good for your brand, and, no pressure, but if you and Delilah wish to start it up again, you have full support from us here at Infinite to put True Crime with Cee and Dee on hold and go full-time to solve these murders again. What we don't want, however, is for you two to put yourselves at risk so if you feel like it's too dangerous, don't do it.

Let me know what you two decide to do.
Respectfully,
Paul T. Larson, Talent Manager
Infinite Podcasting Group

Too dangerous, I think, ha.

I laugh in the face of danger now. I've already faced down my biggest enemy to date and if he can't take me down, no one can. These people think they're impervious, they think they're superhuman. They're not superhuman at all. Underneath their tough exteriors, they're nothing more than a human meat suit. They have skin that cuts like the rest of us, and blood running through their veins that will spill to the ground under the right circumstances.

I'm almost ashamed to admit that the thought of starting up the *Knock Knock Podcast* again is exciting—it was the most thrilling time of my life so far. I still love podcasting, but it doesn't give me the same thrill as it used to. These days it just feels more like it's a job.

I flip through my apps and go to my text messages. One from my mom telling me to be careful; I quickly reply with you too, love you. But there are two others that are catching my eye and it looks like it's one from each of the killers. Now they're both taunting me at the same time—the problem is, I don't know who is who. The first one reads:

Six more, Cobb. What are you waiting for?

I exit out of that text and quickly flip over to the other one which reads:

I want to watch as your guts spill to the floor.

There isn't a way for me to put them into a group chat, so I respond separately, but with the same text.

What are you two waiting for? Come to Lexington and kill me, if you're up for it. You weak ass bitches.

I pause for a moment and think about if I want to add more to that and piss them off even more. I squint my eyes as I think. How can I get inside of their heads?

As soon as you're in my sight, I'll slit your throats and watch you bleed out like I did with Tom. Maybe Delilah will put

a bullet between your eyes like she did to
Tatum. Come and get us, fuckers.

I finish off my scathing message with a cheeky middle finger emoji, and can't help but chuckle to myself. I set my phone down smugly, feeling like I had completely shut them down.

Taunting serial killers with emojis, I think, what has my life become?

I think about the email from Paul again, pick my phone back up and open up my email app. I press the reply button and type out a simple message.

Paul,

Let's do this.

Sincerely,

Cooper Cobb

Delilah and Riley enter the kitchen at almost the exact same time and look at me.

I think they can see by the look on my face that I'm planning something, but they don't quite know what. They look at me suspiciously.

"We're bringing back the *Knock Knock Podcast* immediately," I say.

They look at one another with fear in their eyes as I smile at them deviously, hoping they think that I have a plan in place, but I don't. I'm flying by the seat of my pants. Again.

"You in this time, Riley?" I say. The fear in his eyes grows tenfold.

PART 2

CHAPTER SIXTEEN

MILAN, OHIO - EIGHT MONTHS AGO
KILLER #1

It's a cool autumn evening. The brisk air feels good on my skin which tingles with the falling temperature and the breeze from the nearby lake. I can smell the distant fires crackling and burning through an orange haze in the dying sun. I hear the sound of thunder rumbling way off in the distance, but it is far enough away that we probably have about a half hour before the rain begins to fall. I look up from my phone toward the sound and see a flash of lightning in the night sky.

I look back down at the phone on my lap and continue watching Cooper Cobb talk. This is the most entertained I've been in quite a while, though this scene unfolding in front of me has become tense and frustrating as hell. I can't seem to look away from it despite how uncomfortable the whole thing has become for me.

This is what happens when you tentatively poke at something frighteningly large and powerful——a juggernaut that bends reality around itself like a blanket over one's shoulders on a chilly fall evening. It manipulates your thoughts until your mind is overtaken with madness. Every time you try to run from it, it corners you slowly until you realize that there is no escape except death. You must confront this monster head on or it will eat you alive.

The *Knock Knock Podcast* has become my newest obsession as of late, and honestly, it's about time someone did something about that lunatic. The local police haven't done anything about it——they closed the case when things got just a little too difficult for them, citing lack of evidence and general futility of their attempts to track him down. Sure, there was very little evidence to go off of, but it looks like Cooper Cobb has solved it on his own with nothing more than sheer willpower.

What the fuck?

I straighten my back in my chair and take a deep, long drag of the cigarette in between my fingers. Did Tatum just pistol-whip Cooper in the back of the cranium? Where did she get a gun? What is happening? I take another long drag and inhale the smoke. If I wasn't already, I'm fully invested now. I watch the screen without blinking and Tatum and Delilah stare at one another until Tatum walks over and whispers something in Delilah's ear.

She must not have hit him hard enough, because within a minute or two—though it felt like much longer—I can see him begin to stir at the very bottom of the screen. The two girls hastily walk over to him before he can adjust his eyesight and stand over him, pointing guns right at his head.

Where the fuck did Delilah get a gun? What the hell is happening?

My heart is racing as I watch the scene take place right in front of my eyes and I briefly pray for the safety of all three of them. I watch Cooper intently as he stands back up. I'm waiting for him to pull out a gun, too, but he doesn't. He simply stands up, does some clicking on his computer, then motions his hand. Delilah and Tatum look at one another, then make their way back to their microphones, though keeping their eyes locked on Cooper, guns still drawn.

I sit and continue to watch with baited breath and chief on my cigarette down to the butt, throw it to the ground, and light another one. They're talking to Tom on the phone. He is spilling his guts to the three of them about what motivated him to kill and that he currently has Cooper's parents held hostage.

BANG!

The gunshot echoes like a thunderclap through the studio and I feel my heart quicken with dread. The screen goes white for a split second, but when it returns, I see an image that leaves me dumbfounded. Tatum's body lays motionless on the ground, her eyes wide open in shock and horror as she stares lifelessly at the ceiling, while Cooper and Delilah stand still with their eyes fixed on her corpse. A crimson puddle spreads out from beneath her body, a reminder of the tragedy that had just occurred. My vision blurs as tears fill my eyes—the sight of Tatum laying there lifeless is too devastating to bear. Yet not one of them make any attempt to call for help or render aid; instead, Delilah breaks the silence by uttering a single sentence in an icy voice: "Let's go save your parents." And with that she turns away from Tatum's body, leaving it behind like a forgotten nightmare.

CHAPTER SEVENTEEN

LEXINGTON, MICHIGAN
KILLER #1
THURSDAY JUNE 22ND

Cooper Cobb and Delilah Carney are the targets, but their recent move to Michigan makes things a little more difficult. We have to move strategically and we have to move quickly. Every second those two are still breathing poses a risk to us. We owe it to Tatum and Tom to take these two down swiftly.

I'm sitting in my hotel room letting my thoughts take me away. At least I have a place of refuge to go. The Cadillac House is a beautiful hotel in Lexington and I'm happy to have found a room here considering it's the start of the summer season. It's the best option I have. Even though I'd much prefer being back in Milan with her, the absolute love of my life, she needs to hold down the fort there while I work on scaring Cooper back to Ohio.

I reach over to the bedside table and grab a folded piece of notebook paper. The page is wrinkled but still intact. I unfold it and read it over for probably the hundredth time since it arrived on my doorstep. Some of the ink was smudged from tears when I first received it. I remember walking out my front door and finding it sitting on the stoop in front of me.

Dear Mr. L.,

If you are reading this letter, it means, unfortunately, that neither Tatum nor myself made it through our battle with Cooper and Delilah. It means that we failed miserably. I'm writing this letter to tell you that I am so fucking sorry I couldn't keep either one of us safe. I'm sorry for everything that the two of us put you through and I am sorry that it had to come to this.

I have one dying wish, if you are willing to hear me out. It would mean the world to the both of us. If you are reading this letter because we didn't make it out alive, I need you to take the reins as the new Knock Knock Killer. I need you to end Cooper Cobb and Delilah Carney. Your anger is there, I know it is, now channel it and kill the two of them. Remember, knock twice, wait for the homeowner, push your way in and kill. Use any means necessary. I promise if you start this, Cooper won't be able to keep his nosy ass out of it.

Thank you and I'll see you on the other side,
Tom A. Langford

I set the letter down as I can feel my eyes beginning to well up with tears again. Grief consumes me and it doesn't feel like it will get better anytime soon. The *only* option is to take down Cooper and Delilah once and for all. I swear to God, even if it's the last thing I do, I will kill them both with my bare hands.

I reach over and grab my phone, then navigate to Cooper's contact and click the button to send a text message. I quickly type out a message—it's now or never, it's time to rip off the bandaid.

`Knock Knock, Cooper and Delilah.`

"Let the games begin," I say out loud.

Promptly, a reply text pops through on my end of the phone, which I had not anticipated.

Who's There?

CHAPTER EIGHTEEN

LEXINGTON, MICHIGAN
KILLER #1

I strive to embody the spirit of Tom in all that I do. His vibrant energy, his relentless ambition, his never-ending tenacity—these are the traits I yearn to attain and adopt within me. To experience the same emotion he felt, to think with the same clarity he did, and to execute his actions with my own intent—this is what I strive for every day.

In the garage, I open a drawer and hear the clanking of metal on metal as the drawer slides on the track. I look down at my collection—my beautiful, beautiful collection. I reach a hand in,grab a handle, and bring it to my face. It's gorgeous; one of the most fantastic pieces of modern-day machining: the Buck 119.

One of my most prized possessions is my bench grinder. Well, not mine. I managed to break into Tom's house one night before the police could empty it out and steal it. It was the only thing I wanted and for this exact reason.

Cooper and his family refused to take care of the house, so the city got a dumpster and threw out all of his belongings, like he never existed, the home became city property and promptly sold. Of course they didn't tell potential buyers *who* had lived there previously.

Anything to make a buck.

I fire up the bench grinder and lightly touch the edge of the blade to it as it spins, watching as sparks fly off of it. It makes me happy, maybe too happy, to watch as the blade gets sharper and sharper. The anticipation of what's to come is overwhelming and I struggle to keep my hands steady as I ensure it's sharp enough for no mistakes to occur.

Tonight's the night.

It's my first time.

Tonight, blood spills and I am on my own.

Cooper needs to know he's not dealing with an amateur like Tom Langford. Tom, who got himself *and* his accomplice killed. Tom, what a moron.

It may be my first murder, but I will make it one to remember.

They don't know who the hell they are messing with this time.

This time is different.

This time is more extreme.

This time, we will kill Cooper Cobb and Delilah Carney for everything they stole from us.

Fuck them, I think, then reach over toward my other work bench and grab my Taurus G3 nine-millimeter pistol. It's not the greatest handgun in the world, but it will get the job done. No more cutting and running. If you're going to be a killer, you need to make sure the job is done. Even if that means stabbing, shooting, burning, decapitating.

This time, the kills will be much more brutal.

CHAPTER NINETEEN

LEXINGTON, MICHIGAN
KILLER #1

I'm not as picky as Tom. I'm not going to research my targets. I don't need to know anything about them. Truth be told, the more you know, the more connected you feel and the more remorseful you feel when you slice into someone or put a bullet into their head. That's why they tell you if you ever find yourself in a situation where someone has a gun to your head, you're supposed to start telling your attacker personal information.

I don't care, though. I'm going to pick a house at random, run in, and attack before the people inside have time to react.

I want to see the panic in their eyes.

I want to see the fear.

The people of Michigan have only *heard* of the Knock Knock Killer; now they get to experience his wrath, his power, his violence.

I look up from my dashboard across the street at the house that I've chosen to target. I know nothing about the people inside. I don't know if it's a single person or a large family. All I know is go for whatever male figure is in the house first, then focus on the others.

The house looks relatively dark, like the family has already gone to sleep, though I can't know that to be certain. I reach into the glove box and pull out my nine-millimeter. I cock it back once, ensuring there is a round in the chamber. I already have the Buck 119 in its sheath—I'm ready to do this. I take a deep breath, and swing open my door.

I run across the street as stealthily as I can and take in the atmosphere around me. I can feel the stickiness of the air from the early summer humidity. It's been abnormally warm for this time of year and I can feel the thickness enveloping my lungs as I run. I'm breathing more heavily than normal, though the smoking doesn't help, I'm sure.

I reach the front door of the home and take a moment to catch my breath. My heart is racing, probably a mix of how out of shape I am and the adrenaline coursing through my veins, then I remember what Tom said to me in the letter:

…knock twice, wait for the homeowner.

I raise my hand which is already balled into a fist, then stop for a moment.

Do I really want to do this?

I don't, but I need to.

I put my hand to the solid wood front door and let it rest for a moment, then pull my fist away, then tap on the door twice.

KNOCK. KNOCK.

I listen intently for footsteps coming to the door, but it's dead silent. I decide to break the rules and raise my hand again, but this time instead of two knocks, I give it four in rapid succession. That's when I hear it. Heavy footsteps coming to the door. I can feel a bead of sweat running down my forehead and my heart begins beating even faster. I hear the deadbolt click as the door is unlocked and swings open. A tall man, about six-foot-four, is standing in front of me and, without thinking, I lower the tone of my voice.

"Knock, knock," I say.

I raise my gun at him and he instinctively raises his hands, but I don't give him a chance.

BANG! BANG! BANG!

I give him three shots directly to the chest and I watch as he falls backward onto the floor with an audible thud. I push my way into the house and start frantically looking around. There has to be more people here, then I spot her. A petite woman walks out from behind a wall and looks at me with fear in her eyes.

Oh, the sense of power that makes me feel.

I raise my gun and point it directly at her face, then I lean to the right and look around her. Three small children are cowering behind her crying and shaking. For a moment I feel regret. I feel sad. I can't let them live without parents—can I kill a child?

BANG! BANG! BANG!

The last child runs as his siblings and mother hit the floor. I chase after him and tackle him to the ground, pull out my knife, raise it above my head, and smile deviously at him.

CHAPTER TWENTY

LEXINGTON, MICHIGAN
KILLER #1
FRIDAY JUNE 23RD

I sit in front of my computer with flightradar24.com pulled up on Google Chrome. I'm watching all the flights go across the United States. I know that Riley Stevens is on one of them headed to Detroit and I know he is coming to see Cooper and Delilah—he's staying with them for two weeks.

Riley is Cooper's best friend and confidant.

Best friend. I scoff at the thought.

What best friend doesn't support you when you're succeeding in life?

What best friend distances themselves from you when they don't agree?

That same best friend, though, *was* there when Cooper needed him the most. He was watching the live stream and knew exactly where they were at every given moment. He knew when Cooper needed him and he knew what he had to do. I guess he is a great friend.

There's a particular flight coming from Ohio that I'm watching as it makes its way into Michigan, then into Detroit Metropolitan Airport. I watch as it ticks along and seems to be slowing. This might be the one and I decide to take my chances.

I pull out my phone and quickly pull up Riley's contact in a message, then feverishly type out a message to him.

Knock Knock, Riley. See you soon.

The message doesn't feel complete, though. I think I need to add a little bit more. This feels more like something Tom would send. I'm not Tom. I need to be a little more threatening. I think for a moment, then begin typing again.

I can't wait to slice Cooper up in front of you.
A smile flashes across my face.

CHAPTER TWENTY-ONE

LEXINGTON, MICHIGAN
KILLER #1

I sit at home and enjoy some peace and quiet; I am thoroughly amused by the news stations that keep repeating the same clips and the same stories over and over and over again.

FAMILY OF FIVE KILLED IN QUINTUPLE HOMICIDE.

The police have no leads—so far, I've thoroughly thwarted them. They've found no evidence. I left nothing behind. Just like Tom, he would be proud of me. Why do I care what he would think? I may be doing this because of his letter, but it was his words that inspired me. I'm not doing this *for* him. I'm doing this for myself. This is for me to gain some closure; I want to feel powerful, I want to feel unstoppable, and for once in my life, *I* want to be feared.

I reach over to the side table to my right and grab my pack of Marlboro Red cigarettes. I pull one out of my pack, being careful not to grab the one I've flipped upside down as my "lucky" cigarette, a habit I picked up in high school.

I bring the stick to my mouth and hold it lightly between my lips as I bring my lighter up and deeply inhale the first drag, hold it for a moment, then let it out, closing my eyes and letting any anxiety melt away from my body.

Then, my phone vibrates. I look over and see it lighting up, the name Cooper Cobb flashes on the screen quickly and I stop what I'm doing. My eyes widen and I can't believe what I'm seeing.

Is he really texting me back?

The screen fades to black and I can't bring myself to reach over and pick it up. Tom was right, Cooper will not keep his nosy ass out of this, though, maybe I shouldn't have taunted him.

No. I needed to. I needed to keep things as similar as I could.

I continue sitting and staring at my phone, my hand with the cigarette in it floating in front of my mouth as if I've forgotten how to smoke one. My hand begins to shake—I can't believe he's having this much of an effect on me. This is what I wanted right? We need revenge. Tom and I both need it, even though he isn't here to enjoy it.

With a struggle, I bring the cigarette to my mouth and take a long, deep inhale, bringing the smoke directly into my lungs. The relieving effect of the nicotine hitting the bloodstream isn't working anymore and for every second that passes without reading the message, the shaking of my body intensifies. I need the adrenaline that I felt last night to come back because right now I feel like a total pansy.

The screen lights up again to remind me I have a message. I reach for the phone slowly, trying to calm the shaking. I pick up the phone and swipe to the left to open the message.

`If you want to kill me, come and get me.`

Did he taunt Tom like this, too? I wonder if this is just what this arrogant asshole does or if this is something new. Maybe fighting and winning against Tom gave him some sort of power, too.

Did it?

Is he going to be an even stronger adversary than I thought? Did I underestimate him?

Think.

I can't ignore it. I have to do something. What would Tom do?

Then it dawns on me. I click the contact photo and click the phone button. My thumb hovers over his phone number for a moment. Should I call or text? Calling feels more appropriate. I haven't done that yet. I click his phone number and the line rings a handful of times.

This idiot must be shitting bricks right now, I grin sinisterly, then the ringing stops and silence fills the phone line for a moment.

"What," Cooper says forcefully, trying to sound confident.

"In due time," I say, then quickly hang up the phone.

I bring the cigarette back to my lips and lean back in my chair with a smile on my face.

CHAPTER TWENTY-TWO

MILAN, OHIO
KILLER #2

It's almost my turn to exact revenge on the podcast pair Cooper Cobb and Delilah Carney. He says my time is coming and I am ready for it. I toss my Buck 119 up and down, flipping it as it flies into the air and catching it by the handle. I've practiced working with knives for the last couple of months and I've become fairly good at it if I do say so myself.

I keep flipping the knife around and my eyes squint more and more like a blood-crazed lunatic.

Oh, wait.

The knife comes back down, lands in my hand, and immediately I cock back and chuck the knife at the wall like I'm at the bar playing darts, but this is no game. The blade of the knife sticks into the wall right between the eyes of a printed photo of Cooper. That's how I'm going to do it. I'm going to stab him right between the eyes and watch the blood flow out of his skull as his brain swells and has nowhere else to push it to.

I walk up to the photo and stare at it as though I'm staring directly into his eyes and rip the knife out of the wall.

"Fuck you, Cooper Cobb," I say out loud as my voice shakes, "you're a piece of shit."

His photo grins at me with that normal, cocky grin of his.

I dig my phone out of my pocket without tearing my eyes away from the wall, instead moving to another target: Delilah.

"You're going down, too, bitch," I say.

I look down at my phone, open my text message app, and type out a message.

Knock Knock from Milan, Delilah.

It doesn't feel right—I need to add more. Then, I start typing again.

Start planning your funerals.

Yes. That feels right.

I look back up at the photos and grin again. I feel a fire burning in my soul. It's a fire that no amount of water will be able to put out and I don't want it to. I need my revenge. I need to take my anger out on them.

I need to kill Cooper Cobb and Delilah Carney. But first, a few warnings.

CHAPTER TWENTY-THREE

MILAN, OHIO
KILLER #2

I sit in my car and admire the sunset as it falls beyond the horizon. I can't remember the last time I actually sat and enjoyed the beauty of nature. It's gorgeous. The air is sticky, though, with the early summer humidity.

I'm sitting on the same street where Tom killed the Roberts family—the ones that set everything into motion. I'm sitting in front of a quaint little family home; a modest ranch. I can see the family moving around inside. It seems the town of Milan has already forgotten about the Knock Knock Killer. It's almost night time and their curtains are wide open. I can see everything that's going on inside.

I turn to my left and observe the Roberts home. It hasn't even been listed and I'm curious to know if all of their belongings are still inside or if they've been cleaned out. I wonder if the family even wants to attempt to sell it. The entire country knows what happened there. Would they be better off selling it to the bank and letting them deal with it? Probably.

I look back to the right and study the home that I'm about to break into, or be let into, rather. The sun is almost completely gone and it's almost go-time. I pull out my phone and send out a quick text, then promptly put it back in my pocket. The anticipation is building in my body and I begin to shake and my heart is beating so hard it feels like it might break through my chest and bounce on my dashboard. The sun feels like it's falling much faster now.

I can see light flashing inside the home. The three inhabitants are sitting on the couch and the flashing must be the

TV. They'll be distracted enough, it seems, that I'll be able to take them off guard. That's exactly what I want—it's what I need.

As dusk turns to night, a sudden pit opens up in my stomach. It feels like my intestines are twisting around on themselves and nausea hits. I can feel my dinner working its way up my esophagus. I attempt to open my mouth to take a deep breath, but it seems there is no stopping it. I reach over and grab an ALDI grocery bag and throw it over my face just in time as I heave the contents of my stomach out of my body. Anxiety fills my entire body. As I wipe my face with the clean part of the bag, my hands begin to shake and my heart begins to race and a slight bout of dizziness hits my head.

I can't let fear take me down now that I've made it this far. I'm right here and I'm ready for it. I turn and look back at the house. Darkness has almost completely enveloped the neighborhood now and I know it's almost time. My phone begins to vibrate and I look down.

I'm counting on you. Don't let me down.

I can't.

I won't.

I need to do this. For you. For them.

I reach over to the glove compartment and grab my knife, my gun, and another knife…just in case. I slide on my ski mask to conceal my identity, and get out of the car. Now here I'm standing almost in the middle of the road, a single flickering, dim street light above me illuminating me, but not enough that I'll be seen, and I'm staring at their house. Adrenaline is coursing through my veins and my heart races even faster. I feel like I'm a stand-in for the poster for *The Exorcist*.

Before my brain can process what's happening, my legs begin to move forward and walk toward the house. It doesn't feel like I'm controlling them. It feels like they're moving all on their own, like I'm possessed by something, and before I know it I'm at the front door.

I close my eyes, inhale deep through my nose, exhale slowly out my mouth, and knock on the door.

KNOCK.

KNOCK.

I listen and I can hear footsteps making their way to the door almost immediately. *Or maybe it's my heart beating in my ears*, I think.

Then I hear the lock slide inside the door and I await anxiously for them to open the door. It's now or never. If they open the door and I run, I'm caught for sure. The homeowner opens the door slowly, peeking through a small crack in the door. Clearly they've become a little anxious about the Knock Knock Killer.

The man and I make eye contact and stare at one another. Through the small opening, I can see his eyes darting from my face—or what he can see of it—to my hand holding the knife and my other hand holding the gun.

"C…can I help you?" He asks, his voice shaking with pure fear.

Something about the tone in his voice shakes me to my core, but it's not regret. I'm not considering walking away. It's adrenaline, it's power; I feel like a god. A smile curves at the corners of my mouth, then becomes larger and more sinister and my eyes take on a new ominous shape. I can feel it in the muscles in my face.

"Knock, Knock," I say. As I wind up the man attempts to slam the door closed in my face, but I lean back and quickly ram it with my shoulder. The door swings open and knocks him to the ground. I rush in and look into the living room. The fear on his son's face invigorates me. His wife's scream, oh the scream, it makes me feel good. I stand over the man and he gives me a pleading look, begging for his life without even saying a word. I swing my knife down and stab, pull it out of him, and stab again. I just keep stabbing. I feel like I'm blacked out, like something has completely taken over my body.

I pull the knife out one more time and I stare at him as he writhes in pain, still begging me with his eyes to stop, but I've already stabbed him nine times. I can't stop now. I can't let him suffer. I look down at him and cock my head to the side.

"You didn't say 'who's there?'" I say as I swing the knife down one more time and stab him through his left eye socket. I rip the knife out and I hear him take one last deep breath, then exhale, then nothing. I turn around and look at the wife and son.

"You're next." I say as I point my knife at them and walk toward them slowly like a predator stalking its prey.

CHAPTER TWENTY-FOUR

MILAN, OHIO
KILLER #2
SATURDAY JUNE 24TH

Last night was a rush. Holy shit, was it an amazing experience. I want to believe that I was thorough. I want to hope that I did everything right and that I left no DNA behind. It seems to be pretty easy to evade the Milan Police Department. Tom and Tatum were idiots and they did it.

Tatum, I think, *God dammit, Tom.*

I'm sipping coffee out of my favorite mug that I got from Spirit Halloween. Not your typical coffee mug, it has the Ghostface mask on it. It's my favorite. Just like *Scream* is my favorite horror movie and, like someone that's a huge fan, I know that our kills need to be way more extreme than Tom's. I think I did a good job of it. I just hope *he's* proud of me.

Just as I think about this, my phone begins to vibrate. I look down to see who it is that's calling, but just as I'm about to slide to answer the call, I change my mind and let it ring through to voicemail. About ten seconds later, a message pops up on the screen.

```
Good job last night. I'm proud of you,
hon.
```

A smile curves at the edges of my mouth again and a tear rolls down my cheek. I'm so happy he said it to me; he's never told me he's proud of me before. I was always the second thought, but I'm happy he's involving me and trusting me to take care of things here.

We decided to take the attacks to Lexington and Milan. We need to lure Cooper back here. We need to finish what Tom started and we need to put an end to Cooper Cobb and Delilah Carney.

We need to attack in Lexington to push him back to his hometown and, just when he least expects it, we hit him right where it hurts.

We have to hope and pray that he doesn't watch too much of the news. If he has even the slightest inkling that the attacks have started here again, he won't come back. He will hunt down the Lexington killer and without one another, we can admit that we might be powerless against both of them. We both need to be there and we both need to take them down.

I'm watching the coverage of the carnage I created and I'm proud of myself, too, but pride in myself is nothing compared to his pride in me. I go to my recent calls log and click the last number that called me. It only rings a couple of times, then an answer.

"Well, hello," he says, acting like he didn't *just* call me and wasn't expecting my call. I roll my eyes.

"Hi," I say with a shyness to my voice. I don't really want to talk to him, but I'm warming up to the idea.

"Are you safe?" he asks.

"Yes," I reply.

"You did a good job, sweetie. I'm proud of you,"

"Thank you."

"Now, let's lure him back to Milan," he says. I can hear pure evil in the tone of his voice.

He pauses the conversation for a moment and on his end of the phone, I hear a car door slam.

"What are you doing?" I ask.

"Give me a minute," he replies.

All I can hear is silence and a little bit of static which draws out for a while. I try asking him a few more times what's going on, but he ignores me. About ten minutes go by, then the line is silent and I hear the click of the gearshift being put into park. My heart starts racing and a bead of sweat starts to form at my hairline. I reach an arm up and wipe it away. I'm about to ask him again what the hell is going on when he finally speaks up.

"Text Cooper, now." He says.

"W-what?" I ask. I'm confused. Did he just drive over to spy on Cooper and Delilah?

"Text him now. Remember Detective Carpenter? He just left their house. They're up to something. He needs to be scared. We can't have the authorities involved."

I pull the phone away from my ear and the sweat on my hands makes it difficult to swipe up on my iPhone, exit the call app, and open the messages app, but eventually I get it and hastily type a message. The only thing I can think of right now.

See you in Milan.

CHAPTER TWENTY-FIVE

LEXINGTON, MICHIGAN
KILLER #1

"Pick a house and destroy them," I say just before I angrily slam down the phone. My blood is boiling hot; I feel like a volcano just before it spews piping hot lava. I want to yell, I want to curse, I want to hit something. I want to *kill* something…or someone.

What if? I think about it for a moment. What if she hits another family in Milan and I hit another here in Lexington on the same night? That's something Tom never did and the goal here is to one-up him—to make him look like an amateur, when in reality, we are the amateurs. From what I can feel, though, we are already doing better than him. Maybe not in quantity, but in quality and in extremity.

A full-toothed smile flashes across my face as I imagine law enforcement in two different states trying to find who is responsible and how the person could have possibly gotten away with two murders in one night.

I come back from my daydream and remember that I'm still out in front of Cooper and Delilah's house. I check my surroundings to make sure I'm not being watched when I see Detective Carpenter speeding away in front of me. I think for a moment. We don't need him getting in the middle of this and fucking it up. I pull away from the side of the road where I'm parked and start to follow him.

I need to get rid of him. I need to make sure he can't help Cooper. The police were useless last time, but we don't want to risk someone with experience getting involved—they might figure it out this time. I speed behind him, but keep enough distance to make sure I don't alert him to the tail. He turns and I turn, still keeping a solid distance between us.

This isn't how Tom would want this done.

I shake the thought out of my brain. I don't give a flying fuck what he would think. I'm doing this not simply because he asked, but because I have a reason to do it. I need to send a message to Cooper. I need him to know that his time is coming. We need to do this *like* Tom did, but not exactly like he did it. He got himself and Tatum killed—that won't happen to us.

He turns and I turn again, and he pulls into a parking lot at the beach. What could he possibly be doing here? His is the only car in the lot; this may be my only chance to do this. As I slowly pull into the parking lot behind him, I watch as he gets out of his car, walks up to a park bench, and takes a seat, seemingly just enjoying the nice weather we are getting for once. It's been chilly here and it still is unseasonably cold and definitely not warm enough for a swim. It explains why there's no one else here.

I reach into the glove box and grab my trusty nine-millimeter. It's now or never. I roll down the passenger side window and slowly crawl to a halt, my brakes creaking and squealing as I come to a stop. I'm caught for sure. He's going to hear it and turn around. But he doesn't. He continues to sit without a care in the world staring out into Lake Huron. I raise the gun as my hand shakes like a leaf in the wind. I'm not sure I'm a good enough shot that I'll be able to get him at this distance. I need to get him closer to me somehow. He's going to see my face. Wait. What's that matter? I'm going to *kill* him.

I put the car in park and almost throw myself out of the seat and into the parking lot.

Am I really doing this?

I frantically look around me to ensure no one else has shown up. There's no one here. It's just him and me—this should be easy.

"Hey, Detective," I yell before I can even think about doing it. The words seemed to fly from my mouth.

He jumps, clearly not expecting me behind him, and turns around to look at me and begins to get up from the table.

"How can I help you?" he asks, putting a hand on his holster. He hasn't seen the firearm in my hand yet.

"Come here," I say.

He slowly steps in my direction taking small, deliberate steps, being cautious of what he is about to walk into. I stare at him and don't say anything more.

"Show me your hands," he yells, hand still on his department issued gun. He hasn't raised it at me yet, still just walking toward me. Almost. Just a moment more—just a few more steps and he will be in range.

"I need your help," I yell at him trying to sound desperate and afraid, hoping it kicks his helpful instincts into high gear.

"Sir, I need you to show me your hands," he says again, more forcefully this time.

Two more steps.

One. Two. I raise my firearm and point it in his direction, and he quickly unholsters his and points it at me. He's not afraid to shoot someone. I can tell by the look in his eyes, even though he's a good fifteen paces ahead of me. Something tells me he won't hesitate to pull the trigger.

"Put the weapon down!" he shouts. His voice echoes through the air and the sound waves bounce off the water behind him and back to me quickly.

I give him my new signature grin then say the two little words that strike fear into his heart.

"Knock, knock."

I quickly pull the trigger and can see his eyes widen before the bullet rips through his chest and a small splatter of blood shoots out as he falls to the ground. His firearm flies through the air and lands a good ten feet behind him. He's still conscious and is trying to reach it, but the pain coursing through his body is too severe as he clutches his chest and blood begins to pool on his shirt.

I walk up to him and look him right in the eyes as he tries to form a coherent sentence. It looks like the bullet went right through his heart so he is finding it difficult to breathe. I raise my gun one more time, firing another round directly into the middle of his forehead.

CHAPTER TWENTY-SIX

MILAN, OHIO
KILLER #2

`I killed him.`

The text reads ominously, but I don't know what he's talking about at all. Did he take down Cooper? Did he kill Riley? I shudder to think about it. I quickly hit the contact at the top of the screen and hit the phone icon to call him. I need to know. It rings and rings and rings. Just when I think it's about to go to voicemail, silence fills the line.

"Hello?" I question nervously.

"Hi," he says.

"Who did you kill?"

Silence fills the phone line again and I can hear him breathing heavily. I try to remain calm—I need to. It's clear to me that he is freaking out. Quietly, I start to panic on the inside, too. If he didn't stick to the plan, we are so screwed. I can feel my heart racing which causes my lungs to feel stuck and unable to move in my chest. I try to keep my breaths controlled and subtle. I wonder how an orange jumpsuit will look on me.

"I killed…" he starts, "…the detective."

"Carpenter?" I scream at the top of my lungs. The fear in my voice is unmistakable. "This isn't how we rehearsed things," I yell again, "you weren't supposed to kill a damn cop."

"I did what I had to. He was meddling," he replies, still trying to catch his breath.

I pace back and forth and put my hand to my forehead. I'm stressing now and I don't think I can control the panic attack that's coming on. As dizziness hits me, I sit down on the couch. I have to, or I will pass out and slam down to the floor. I can't do that right now.

"What are we going to do?" I ask.

"Nothing. I left his body. They're going to find him dead, they won't be able to identify that it came from my gun. It's all going to be okay."

Nothing will ever be okay again.

"But I need to ask you another favor," he says.

"What?" I ask.

"We kill again tonight," he says insistently.

"What do you mean 'we'?" I ask. He's in Lexington, I'm in Milan. Is he coming back?

"I'm killing here, and you're killing there. Same night. Let's really throw things off and derail their investigation before it barely even starts."

What he's proposing is lunacy, but I don't dare question him. He's insane—completely lost his mind.

"Okay," I say, "let's do this."

CHAPTER TWENTY-SEVEN

LEXINGTON, MICHIGAN
KILLER #1
SUNDAY JUNE 25TH

It's morning and the sun is shining bright in the sky. It's filtering through my front window and when you pair that with the sound of waves crashing against the shoreline, it creates an atmosphere of pure bliss. Solitude, peace, whatever you want to call it. It's wonderful. There are several others that can't say the same this morning. Six more people across two states did not wake up this morning, thanks to us.

I'm standing at the kitchen sink. I don't know what happened last night. I must have come home and the adrenaline must have knocked me unconscious. I have dried blood drops on my face that I'm now having to wash off. I try to replay the night before, but all I remember is walking in and immediately grabbing a glass of whiskey to hide the pain I feel for everything we are doing.

That's it.

I must have drank a little more than I thought; that's probably what knocked me out. I didn't do anything when I got home except fix myself a glass of whiskey. It starts to come back to me. Then another and another and another. Glass after glass, not even savoring the flavor. I might as well have been doing shots. I finish cleaning myself off then look at the rest of my skin: my arms, legs, hands. It doesn't seem like there is anything left on me, thankfully.

I go to sit in my oversized Gardner White recliner and sigh, all the while reaching over and grabbing a cigarette out of my pack, lighting it, and taking a deep inhale. I grab the remote and turn on the TV. I know what I'm going to see, but the confirmation makes me feel something. It makes me feel good—it almost makes me feel famous.

Flipping through the channels I can see that our actions have made national news now. They're covering both the murders in Milan and in Lexington. I love it, it makes me feel powerful, and any ounce of regret I felt immediately disappears. I know I need to do something now to make sure Cooper knows this isn't a game. We will surpass Tom's body count. We've killed fourteen people now. We are almost halfway there at this point. I intend on making Cooper and Delilah the ones that send us flying past the goal. That's the plan, anyway.

I pick up my phone and instruct my partner to text Cooper at the same time as me. She confirms that she will.

I bring up his contact and consider what to say. It needs to be perfect.

Six more, Cobb. What are you waiting for?

The words flow from my fingers onto the keyboard without too much effort or thought behind it. The problem is I know this cocky asshole is going to text back—he always does.

What are you two waiting for? Come to Lexington and kill me, if you're up for it. You weak ass bitches.

I laugh loudly as I read his words. I'm not afraid of him. Who does he think he is? Then, another text pops through.

As soon as you're in my sight, I'll slit your throats and watch you bleed out like I did with Tom. Maybe Delilah will put a bullet between your eyes like she did to Tatum. Come and get us, fuckers.

That one cut like a knife. No pun intended.

"Fuck you, Cooper," I say as a tear runs down my face which I wipe away quickly. I don't do that. This motherfucker will pay for everything he's done—him *and* that little bitch.

CHAPTER TWENTY-EIGHT

MILAN, OHIO
KILLER #2

It's been a few days and I haven't heard one single syllable out of him. He won't text me, he won't call me. I know he is still alive because I can watch him moving around on Life360. I'm staring at it right now. I can see his indicator moving at a fairly high rate of speed.

What could he be doing?

I watch as he stops randomly and the icon jumps around a little bit but mostly stays centralized in one particular place. I don't know why, but just the fact that I can see it moving makes me feel okay. I wouldn't know what to do if I lost him, especially right now. We've made it too far and, though I know the finish line is way off in the distance, it feels like we are quickly closing the gap.

I choose to distract myself and listen to a podcast; maybe it will help me focus on something else for a little while. When I open Apple Podcasts, something catches my eye and I can't believe I never removed it from my favorites list. The *Knock Knock Podcast* is sitting right in front of my face. I'm reminded of that night: the night that I discovered PTSD and anxiety, the night I watched two people die on camera. It was horrific, it was terrifying, but now I'm the one whose hands people die by. It's ironic, really, and therapeutic.

If I had a therapist I'd be in a padded room for sure.

I click the podcast and notice something strange. A new episode has been uploaded. I furrow my brows and cock my head slightly to the right like a dog does when you ask if they want to go for a walk, but more inquisitive. I debate for a moment whether I want to go to the episodes list and see what it's all about, then, as if I didn't think about it at all, I click and the episode starts playing.

The old introduction music is nostalgic, though they've only been off the air for a few months. It takes me back to good times, even though I associate the podcast with nothing but sadness and fear at the same time.

PTSD is a real confusing bitch.

I don't really know what I was hoping for, but the next thing I hear stuns me. It makes me freeze in place and my heart start pumping so hard I can hear every beat in my ears. I think I was hoping it was an old unaired episode being uploaded, but it's not. As soon as I hear them talking, I know it's not because there is something new here, something that I've never heard before being said.

"Welcome to the new *Knock Knock Podcast*," Cooper starts. His voice sends chills up my spine. "I'm your host, Cooper Cobb."

"And I'm Delilah Carney," Delilah says in her arrogant, bitchy tone of voice.

I can't seem to get sound to come out of my voice box, so I just mouth the words "you bitch," then listen intently.

"And for his very first time on the show," Cooper says as if he is building up to something dramatic.

"I'm Riley Stevens," Riley, Cooper's best friend, says.

I jump up and yell. "What the hell?"

PART 3

CHAPTER TWENTY-NINE

DELILAH CARNEY
THURSDAY JUNE 22ND

All I can do is sit on the toilet seat and stare down at the test that is staring back up at me. Figuratively, of course, but I feel like it's staring into my soul with piercing eyes waiting for me to make a decision. What will that decision be? I know what Cooper would want from me and I know deep down what I want, but is this really a good time with a potential copycat killer coming around?

A tear rolls down my cheek from my left eye and my right eye begins to flood too and I'm not sure if they are happy tears, sad tears, mad tears, or something else. I'm feeling so many emotions right now that I can't tell which is the dominant one. I'm sad because I always dreamt of having a kid and making my parents grandparents, but they won't be—ever. I'm happy because I know I'm having a kid with the best man I've ever met, and I'm mad because I know what kind of evil world we would be bringing this kid into.

I take a deep breath and consider how I'm going to tell Cooper. I can't tell him right now, that would distract him and there's too much to do. I stand up, raise my shirt, and look down at my stomach. I start to imagine a giant stomach where my normally mostly flat stomach is. I picture the pouch that I might be left with at the bottom after my uterus goes back into place. The longer I stare, the longer I think I'm already showing.

No.

I know I'm not—I'm way too early into this to be showing quite yet. Six weeks, maybe? I need to see a doctor or maybe the stress from whatever may be coming will cause a miscarriage. I don't want that, but it's a possibility. Every little thought about what could go wrong is quickly running through my head, shuttering any chance of a good thought to sneak its way past. I don't want to focus on the negative. The last few months have been great. It finally felt like life was moving in the right direction after a few missteps.

After everything that went down with Tom, I spent a week being held in the Erie County Jail in Sandusky while law enforcement reviewed everything that happened. I never actually killed anyone—well, except for Tatum, and I agreed to team up with Tom for one simple reason: to protect Cooper. After the police reviewed the footage from that night, after the longest week of my life, they let me go and deemed the murder an act of self-defense. I was thankful for that, I still am. I can't get involved this time except with Cooper. That's it; no teaming up with the killer, if it actually is one and not just a prankster.

As I stare at the test in my hand that is now leaking urine out into my palms, I hear a voice outside the bathroom door.

"Delilah, are you okay in there?" Cooper asks.

"I'm fine," I say with a panic-laced tone, "just give me a minute."

I can hear him walking away. One thing that's good about Cooper is he never questions me and takes everything I say at face value.

BUZZ.

My phone vibrates on the counter and I look down at it as if it has something to say. I want to ignore the notification because the fear of who might be trying to reach me is always there, lingering in the back of my mind. It could be something and it could be absolutely nothing. Hell, it could just be Facebook or Instagram or one of the other million social media sites I use, but still, that nagging feeling in the back of my brain remains.

BUZZ.

It vibrates again and I continue to stare at it, but another thought enters my mind. I look down at the plastic in my hand. How the hell am I going to hide this from Cooper? Then, as if a lightbulb lights up over my head, I have an idea. I reach under the sink and aimlessly reach my hand in search of a box. I finally find my box of tampons, pull one out of the plastic wrapper, wrap it in toilet paper, and toss it in the garbage. Then I carefully slide the test into the tampon wrapper, make sure it is not visible, and toss that in the garbage. I wad up a few more pieces of toilet paper and throw them on top for good measure.

I stare at the garbage for a moment, debating if that's where I'm going to keep it hidden. Shit. No. He will find it, I'm sure. I immediately dig it back out of the trash can and stuff it into my pocket. I need to think more clearly but I'm panicking.

BUZZ.

"Dammit, what do you want?" I say as I hastily grab my phone and turn it around, unlocking the screen with my face. I don't even notice the contact name as I do this and simply pull up the message which takes me by surprise.

My face drops and my jaw feels like it's going to fall off and hit the tile floor. My eyes widen as I read the message. This can't be real. There's no way this is real. I squeeze my eyes shut for a moment, hoping I simply wake up in my bed when I reopen them, but as I carefully open one eye at a time, I realize I'm not dreaming. I am, in fact, awake.

It's not an unknown number this time. It's a contact I have saved in my phone which I forgot was even in there. I can't believe I never deleted it, but I definitely will now. The name Tom is sitting at the top of the screen. There's no way. How in the shit does someone have his phone? This might be a good thing for us, though. Now I can't delete the contact, right? I read the text.

`Hi Delilah, care to join me?`

Without thinking, I type out the best message I can think of at this very moment. It's quick and to the point, but I don't want to hide any secrets this time around. I'm not sneaking around on Cooper again—I hated everything about that. I felt like I betrayed him, even though he understood why I did it and he never holds it against me.

`Fuck you. Lose my number.`

CHAPTER THIRTY

DELILAH CARNEY
FRIDAY JUNE 23RD

My eyes pop open suddenly and I'm met with nothing but darkness. They dart back and forth as if I'm unaware of where I am, but I know I'm lying in my bed. I can feel Cooper's presence next to me and, as if that isn't enough, I can hear him snoring like a freight train.

I rub my face a little bit, then decide if I'm awake I might as well get out of bed. My stomach is rumbling in agitation. It's flipping all over the place and prompts me to throw myself out of bed and run to the bathroom. I open the toilet seat with such force that it slams against the tank. I squeeze my eyes shut tight in response to the clangor, then open one eye, listening intently for Cooper to wake up. He doesn't.

As I stand above the toilet, the nausea in my stomach intensifies and I begin to gag a little bit. If this is going to happen, it's better for it to be while he's asleep. I don't need to explain this to him right now. He doesn't need to know yet and, luckily, I'm a quiet puker.

Just come out already.

As if my stomach listened to my command, I heave into the toilet, but nothing comes out except water and a little bit of bile. I'll take that over solid food any day. I finish and take a moment to catch my breath, then flush the toilet, head over to the sink, and brush my teeth.

Cooper should be up soon, so I sneak as quietly as I can out of the bedroom and onto the stairway, ensuring I avoid the one extremely loud step as I descend. Immediately, I make my way over to the coffee maker, start brewing a pot, and eagerly await the caffeine rush I so desperately need right now. Instead of sitting and staring at the slow-dripping pot, I sit on the couch, rest my head against the cushion, and close my eyes for a moment.

***

I know this place, I think.

I look around and notice I'm in a cemetery. The details aren't quite complete and everything around me is fuzzy, but I get this feeling that I'm familiar with the scenery. I begin to walk and start noticing out-of-focus stones littering the ground, but I can't make out the words on them until I come across one in particular. It's a beautiful, glossy black marble headstone with silver engraving. I recognize it immediately. The last name Carney is written in big bold letters. I'm standing at my family's gravesite.

I bend down and run my fingers along the engraving. How I wish I could see them one more time. I miss them so much. It's been almost four years since they were taken from me and, though it gets easier as time passes, I miss them more and more every day.

The ground beneath me begins to rumble and as I look around trying to figure out what's happening, I see other headstones moving in on me. I notice the last name on another one and it reads Roberts—the Roberts family who lost their lives to the Knock Knock Killer. I can't help but think we inadvertently caused their deaths.

I stand back up and look around as I'm being closed in on, then, in the distance, a shadow appears; nothing more than a silhouette, but I squint my eyes hoping it'll somehow help me see the person a little better. It doesn't, but a nagging feeling in the back of my mind tells me I know who it is. I don't want to admit it, but I do know who it is.

I hear voices around me. They're distant, but there's no mistaking they're there. I can't make out what they're saying, but they sound sinister, deadly, threatening. The shadow suddenly seems to teleport out of the darkness right in front of me and I'm face to face with Tom Langford, the original Knock Knock Killer. He is almost pressing his nose to mine. His deadly eyes stare into mine as though he's trying to steal my soul. He just stares for what feels like forever, but then he opens his mouth.

"Join me," he says with a hoarseness to his voice that wasn't there while he was alive.

I glance down and see the slash across his throat from when Cooper killed him and blood is pouring out of it. I look back up at him.

"Kill with me, my love," he says.

I open my mouth to tell him not to call me that, but no words come out.

I scream and suddenly everything disappears.

***

My eyes open again and light is beginning to shine through the living room windows. The whole house is filled with the scent of freshly brewed coffee. I must have been out for at least an hour. I reach up and rub my face again, but this time I have sweat dripping from my hairline down my face.

I get up and walk to the kitchen, grabbing a paper towel to quickly wipe the moisture from my face. I shake off the nightmare and make myself a cup of coffee.

What the hell was that?

I walk back to the couch and sit down with my coffee and take in the fragrance of the hazelnut creamer I put in it mixed with the light scent of the beans. I'm not Cooper. I don't do black coffee whatsoever; it looks like mud and tastes way too bitter. I have to have some flavor to it.

I grab the remote and turn on the TV, flipping from channel to channel until I get to the local news. There's not much on that I want to watch so I leave it there. As I sit back enjoying my coffee, the breaking news report graphic pops on screen and cuts to the anchors sitting in the studio. Normally I don't put too much stock in these breaking news reports, but after the texts and the nightmare, my eyes are fixed on the screen.

The anchors are talking about an attack that turned deadly right here in Lexington. It's out of the ordinary here from what I can tell. We haven't been here very long, but it seems like a mostly peaceful lakefront town where nothing bad ever happens.

"Quintuple homicide," the anchorwoman says, which grabs my attention even more. I lean forward as if being able to see the TV closer will help to ensure I am, in fact, hearing what I think I'm hearing.

"No leads at this time," she continues to say—it feels all too familiar.

"Stabbed to death," she continues as I only catch and hang on to certain words as she is speaking.

"Shot with a nine-millimeter handgun," she says, which piques my interest further.

"Two adults and three children," she continues describing the brutal attack.

It's really feeling like…

"No signs of forced entry, the husband was found dead just inside the front door, which was cracked open when police arrived," she says, which confirms exactly what I was thinking.

I practically jump off the couch and go airborne. I run around, basically throwing my coffee mug down on the kitchen island. Coffee splashes all over the counter, but I'm already halfway to the stairs. I run up them two at a time, not caring about the insanely loud steps. As I reach the top, I almost crash through our bedroom door where I'm met with Cooper standing in the middle of the room, eyes wide from the impact.

"You…need…to…come…see…this," I say, breathing between every word trying to bring air back into my lungs.

CHAPTER THIRTY-ONE

DELILAH CARNEY

In all of the time I've known Cooper, I've never been one to keep anything from him. He's my best friend, and now my fiancé—I tell him everything. Sure, there was that whole teaming-up-with-a-killer-and-accepting-dirty-money-to-protect-him thing, but that was for his own good. Now I'm keeping two secrets from him: the fact that I am pregnant with his child, and that the new killer is texting me. I don't want him to worry and I know that either of these secrets would do exactly that, worry him.

I stare out the window the entire way to the airport to pick up Riley. I can't bring myself to hold a conversation with Cooper. I'm afraid if I open my mouth, everything will come rushing out of my mouth like a dam that's broken open, flooding everything.

My phone buzzes and I quickly click the lock button on the side of the device to keep him from hearing it. I don't think he will, anyway; he's in his own world listening to Ice Nine Kills. I briefly glance over at him from the corner of my eye, but he is fully engrossed in "Welcome To Horrorwood." I look back out the window and stare into the distance as cornfields fly past us—rather, we fly past them.

I want to ignore the notification currently taunting my mind, but I can't. My phone buzzes again, reminding me to check it as if it can read my mind and knows that I am struggling to ignore it. I turn the phone over and look at it. It's exactly who I thought it was.

Join me or he dies.

I struggle with these messages now. On one hand, they don't bother me, I got used to it with only a few months of reprieve. But at the same time, it shakes me to my core. Riley is going to lose his absolute shit. He didn't want to get involved last time, and now he's going to be trapped here in this with us. That is, unless he decides to turn his ass right back around and get on a plane back to Ohio.

After a very long drive, we finally pull up and park in the pickup area at the airport. I watch as people from all walks of life run in and out of the front doors—men in business suits, families dragging their kids inside and out for vacation. Lost in my own stupor, Cooper finally breaks the awkward silence between us.

"Dee," he says with a little hesitation in his voice, "I need your opinion. Do I tell Riley or not?"

"I don't know, Cooper," I say, "on one hand, it might be a good idea but on the other, I just don't know."

The real question in my mind is, do I tell Cooper about the texts and the baby growing inside of me? I think when I gave him my answer, I wasn't actually answering his question, but fighting with the thoughts inside my own mind. If this is happening again, if it's *really* happening again, I think I will completely lose my sanity. But I know I can't. If this is happening again for real, I need to be there for Cooper again, just…not in the same way. I won't risk losing his trust again.

Surprisingly, he handled that whole thing really well. Maybe it was the money, maybe it was just that I confessed to everything right away—well not right away, it was a couple of weeks later. I explained to him that Tom reached out to me, not the other way around. I told him that Tom needed an extra set of hands which gave me an advantage. He called me in a fit of desperation and was sure he was going to be caught before he could carry out his final plan. I told him to pay me and he obliged with the entirety of $250,000 in advance. I never did a single thing he told me except bring Cooper to him, but I would have never done that had I thought he didn't stand a chance against Tom. I wouldn't put his life at risk like that.

He begged and pleaded with me to help him and Tatum; I was supposed to be in on the Roberts family murder, but I backed out at the last second—boy, did that piss him off. I thought that was going to be the end for me, but he never came after me. He never attempted to attack me, though I think the knife thrown through the window was definitely aimed at me.

Tom was in love with me and Tatum simultaneously. He was really in love with her, but he had told me on the side that he'd love to be together, that I had a better head on my shoulders than her. I kept up the charade that I had feelings for him, too. It kept me on his good side and I couldn't risk him throwing me under the bus until the timing was just right. It had to be me that revealed my involvement to Cooper.

I continue to watch all of the people rush in and out of the airport, wondering where the hell Riley is. Riley is one of those people who can make conversation with anyone he meets, so, for all we know, he could've just met his new best friend in there and they are chatting it up like they've known each other forever.

I start to panic because I can feel it coming. My mouth fills with saliva, my head gets slightly dizzy, and my stomach begins to turn. I close my eyes and breathe deep, trying to fend off the impending vomit, but quickly realize there isn't anything I can do to stop it. I close my mouth tightly as it flies up my esophagus and into my mouth. I have to try to keep it from Cooper so I do the only thing I can think of.

GULP.

Ugh, gross.

Just then, I hear the latch of Cooper's door open and he's out of the car before I can reopen my eyes. I look over to the doors and see the two of them give one another a bro-hug, but a nagging feeling overcomes my thoughts: this could very well be the last time all three of us hang out. Something feels different this time around already—I don't know what it is, but something tells me we aren't going to be dealing with your run-of-the-mill murderer. This time, it will be worse. Much worse.

CHAPTER THIRTY-TWO

DELILAH CARNEY
SUNDAY JUNE 25TH

It's been a few days since everything started and all seems mostly quiet with the exception of one more household murdered in Lexington and one more in Milan. The murders seem to be getting worse and the more information that comes in, the more grotesque as well. When it comes to the texts and the calls, though, it's been radio silence with the exception of the night we got Riley back to our place. Well, according to my knowledge at least–Cooper hasn't said much about it except for one text taunting him to come back to Milan.

Detective Carpenter visited us yesterday. I think he followed us to Milan. I don't have any evidence to back up that accusation, but why else would he just so happen to start working for the Lexington Police Department? It doesn't make much sense—is he involved somehow? My mind has been racing for the last couple of days trying to make sense of everything happening. It makes me wonder what *we've* done to deserve all of this. Tom was one thing, he just wanted old fashioned revenge, but who the hell did we piss off this time?

It doesn't matter what I think about, whether it's the murders, Cooper, Riley, somehow my brain pulls a U-turn and lands on thinking about the baby. The unplanned, yet already loved little life growing inside of me. I look down at my stomach again, thinking I see a bump forming. Although I know it's not, I still run my hands along my stomach, the motherly instincts deep in the recesses of my brain already coming out. I need to find a way to clear my thoughts.

Yesterday, an agent with the Federal Bureau of Investigation called Cooper and he basically told the agent to go fuck himself. We don't have a great history with law enforcement in this type of situation. They give up too easily whereas Cooper does not—he'd have made a great cop, but his persistence and his inability to let things go probably would have also been his downfall.

Cooper telling off a federal agent is hysterical, though, and the memory creeping back into my mind makes me chuckle to myself. I need a little bit of humor in my life right now.

I'm deep inside my own thoughts when Cooper speaks up, finally.

"We're bringing back the *Knock Knock Podcast* immediately," he says.

Cooper wanting to start up the *Knock Knock Podcast* again is terrifying, yet, for some reason, I agree. I think I miss the thrill of the hunt—the mystery and the "whodunit" aspect of it all. I need a good adrenaline rush.

What if I end up like my sister?

The thought occurs to me out of nowhere and sends chills up my spine. She never had a real chance to start her life and that saddens me. I've only just begun my adult life, and while I've given it a fair shake, what if I don't get to become a mother? A tear runs down my face and I quickly wipe it away before Riley or Cooper can see it.

I need to get out of the house for a little bit. I need to take a walk and I need to clear my mind. It's summer, I should be outside a little more anyway.

"I'm going for a walk," I say suddenly, making Cooper and Riley both look at me confused.

"Is everything okay?" Cooper asks.

"Everything is fine. I just need to clear my head."

"Want me to go—"

I cut him off before he can finish his sentence.

"No, I need to be alone for a little bit," I say, fending off any chance of him following me.

I grab my purse and phone quickly and walk out the door without another word. I know he's going to track my movements. Ever since things went down with Tom, he's been tracking me on Life360. Most people would think it's possessive, but Cooper isn't like that. I know he does it for my safety and I adore him for it.

I take in the sunshine as it beats on my face. A light breeze wafts through the air making the temperature a perfect seventy degrees. The heat feels great and it's as if I haven't stepped outside in months. I almost haven't. Most of our time is spent working on the podcast or in the studio. We are so busy that we don't make as much time for ourselves as we should.

The beach sounds like a great idea, I think.

CHAPTER THIRTY-THREE

DELILAH CARNEY

I pull up to the beach and park my car. I roll the window down to take in the sounds and smells of the lakefront. I close my eyes for a moment and enjoy every second of the peace that Lake Huron has to offer. Beautiful, yes, but can also show the full extent of nature's fury at only a moment's notice. Luckily, today is the former.

I can hear the squawking of seagulls flying overhead and the waves lapping lightly on the shore. I get out of my car and look around for a minute, secretly hoping I'm alone, but knowing the chances are slim. As I observe, I notice I am, in fact, alone on the beach. It's strange; usually tourists are all over the beach, but it's not a great swimming day and it's early in the season. I'm sure the lake would be ice cold.

I walk down to the beach and kick off my flip flops, letting the sand squish between my toes. I slowly walk toward the water, just barely allowing the water to touch my feet. The light waves push up onto shore and, as expected, the water *is* very cold. It makes me flinch but my skin adjusts to the change in temperature quickly.

I stare off into the distance and at the horizon I can see a square object separating the sky from the water. I squint my eyes trying to figure out what it is. It's a freighter. A massive ship that seems to defy all the laws of physics and, despite its massive size, manages to float right on top of the water with little effort as it hauls whatever goods are on board.

I smile. The peace I feel in this moment is unmatched. I haven't felt this way in what feels like forever, though it's only been a handful of months. The experience definitely caused some trauma and anxiety issues, though I rarely show that side of me to Cooper. I always feel like I need to be strong for him, despite the fact he's strong enough for the two of us. Writing the book helped, and, while I try to remain humble about it, it became an instant *New York Times* Best Seller. Although it isn't about the money, I made a ton off of it, which helped me take my mind off of everything that happened. It made the move to Michigan easier, too.

I lie down in the sand and continue to let the water lap at my toes. I stare at the sky and imagine what my family is doing right now, wherever they are. Would they be proud of me? I often wonder about that. I hope they are, but I can almost hear my mom talking to me sometimes. *Dee, don't do anything stupid and reckless. Be smart like I know you are.* The thought makes me smile, my whole life for the better part of a year has been nothing but reckless.

I close my eyes and focus on the sound of the water. It seems like the waves are beginning to crash harder, but I don't feel the wind picking up speed. Through my eyelids, I can see the sunlight fading slowly. Then, seemingly out of nowhere, the sky turns cloudy, then darker and darker until it almost feels like nighttime. I open my eyes and just as I thought, it's pitch black outside and looks like rain is about to start falling any second. Confusion fills my mind as there wasn't a cloud in the sky just a minute ago. I jump up, throw my flip flops back on, and turn around, heading back to the car.

I look up and I'm met with a figure standing maybe fifty feet away from me. They're wearing a black robe with a hood that covers their face. I stop dead in my tracks and stare at them, but they don't do anything. They don't move a muscle, they look like a statue. I inch closer one step at a time and they still don't move. Between every step, I pause and watch, waiting for them to run at me or something worse.

My phone buzzes and I pull it out of my pocket. I look at the screen to see a text message has come through.

I killed him.

That's all it says, but those three words send an icy-cold chill up my spine, making the hairs on the back of my neck stand at attention. Who? Cooper? Riley? I try to open my mouth to scream at the person seemingly staring at me, but as I try to speak, nothing comes out. I put my hands to my mouth and my lips are messily stitched together so I'm unable to open them. Tears begin running down my face and all I can do is whimper from my throat.

The figure then begins to move, not toward me, but slowly raises their right arm and points into the distance. I look in the direction they're pointing, but I see nothing. The wind is whipping around me and I can feel my eyes drying from it. I blink and when I open my eyes, dozens of dead bodies appear from nowhere and are lying all over the beach—all of them stabbed in different ways from single stab wounds to the abdomen to gashes across their throats. I look around at all the bodies piled up and notice one family in particular; the Roberts family with our names still carved into their abdomens. I try to scream again, but it's for naught.

I begin to sob now, but am still unable to open my mouth and scream for help. The most gut-wrenching evil laugh pierces the air around me. It's deep and guttural. I know who the person is now: it's Tom and he's just staring at me, or so I think. But then I feel a presence right next to me and I'm afraid to look, afraid to find out who it is, but I look to my right. I need to know.

Tom is standing next to me with a slash from one side to the other across his throat and I do a double take and the masked figure is still standing across the beach from me.

Wait, if that's Tom, then who is that?

"Delilah Rae, my love," he says as he looks deep into my eyes, giving me a loving look that only a significant other can.

I reach up and rip the stitches out of my mouth as blood begins to pour onto the ground.

"I'm not your love, Tom," I say, "I never was. I'm Cooper's."

He furrows his brows in disapproval and his eyes narrow. I remember that look. I remember the anger and the fire. I can almost see the flames as they grow in his pupils. Just hearing Cooper's name fuels the hatred in his soul.

"Not for long," he says with a laugh, "this isn't over."

Before I'm able to open my mouth to speak again, he disappears in a cloud of smoke. I frantically look around me, but he's nowhere to be found. As if someone is speaking into a microphone, I can hear a voice echoing around me. It's not Tom this time, it's someone else. It's a voice that I know, but I can't quite place it. It's a little distorted and I focus on it the best I can, but my head feels like it's swirling and I feel as though I'm about to fall over.

"It's only just begun," the voice says echoing through the air.

Beginning at the edges, my vision starts to go black and it slowly moves in on me. I collapse to the ground and before long, everything ceases to exist and I slowly drift away.

My eyes snap open and I'm met with intense rays of sun shining into my corneas. I squint at the sight. I'm lying on the beach again and the air is just as still as it was. I must have fallen asleep.

That was a hell of a nightmare.

Panicked, I look all around me, but there's no sign of Tom, no sign of the hooded man. Definitely just a nightmare. I take a few deep breaths and try to control the air going in and out of my lungs until my heart beat slows down to a normal rate again. I get up, slide my flip flops back on, and turn around, heading back to my car.

As I walk back, I see seagulls circling above, squawking almost as if there is a predator nearby. I see a few of them dive bomb to the ground about thirty feet to my left and they land around a mass in the grass. I stare at it for a moment, trying to figure out what it might be.

Is that? I think to myself.

Against my better judgment, I walk over to it, shooing the seagulls away as I get closer and closer. When I get close enough, I recognize it, the one thing I've seen way too much of in my life. A dead body. I run up, having to push some of the more brave seagulls off of the man lying lifeless on the ground. I roll his body over to get a look at his face.

Stupid. Now your fingerprints are on him.

As his extremely large and heavy body rolls, I throw my hands over my mouth and gasp. I know this man and I just saw him, just yesterday—or was it the day before? I can't remember, every day seems to melt together. Either way, Detective Carpenter is lying dead before my eyes.

What should I do?

I do the one thing I can think of, though it probably isn't the right choice. I pull out my phone and dial Cooper immediately. It rings and rings, then goes to his voicemail.

"Fuck," I yell as I attempt to call again. I wanted an adrenaline rush, but not like this. My hands are shaking as I try to select his name.

The phone rings several times and just as I think it's about to go to voicemail again, he answers in the sweet tone that I've learned to love.

"Cooper, I just found Detective Carpenter. He's fucking dead!"

PART 4

CHAPTER THIRTY-FOUR

COOPER COBB

"Welcome to the *new* version of the *Knock Knock Podcast*," I say with excitement in my voice. It's surreal to be back and doing the show that I loved. Admittedly, I've been getting a little burned out on the new show. There isn't any excitement to the show like this has. It's the same thing, day in and day out, just talking about true crime instead of living it. At least this brings meaning to my life.

"And I'm Delilah Carney," Delilah says with a similar exhilaration in her voice, but the look on her face tells me she's not looking forward to this at all. Still, I need to press on. If we are even half as successful as we were before, the revenue will set us up for quite a while, and there's also the whole catching a killer thing.

"And for his very first time on the show," I continue.

"I'm Riley Stevens," Riley says, his face beaming. It's a huge change from the Riley we knew just eight months ago, the one who didn't want anything to do with the show. I think his run-in with Tom when he tackled him in the cemetery gave him the drive to want to help us; plus, he's stuck here and can't get away from it. Either way, I'm happy he's here.

I look behind the glass separating us and the recording booth. Remi, our recording engineer, is sitting down at the mixing board monitoring audio levels and checking everything. He's mostly there to click buttons for us and monitor us for time. That's one thing about being managed by a distributing company: we get monitored for time and we have to limit our episodes.

I look to his right and our manager, Paul Larson is standing next to him with a smile from ear to ear, giving the three of us two thumbs up. Of course he's happy; when we make money, he makes money, and our show makes him stacks of cash. He makes sure we stay on track as well and sometimes gives his input on editing the content to make it more listener-friendly—more entertaining.

Paul is our new manager, too, and he is much better at his job than our last one, Lars. Lars didn't last too long after we took down the Knock Knock Killer. Said, and I quote, "Fuck this," and just took off. No one has seen him since. Infinite can't track him down and he seems to have changed his number. It makes me chuckle everytime I think about it. Paul, on the other hand, is too money-motivated to give up on us and encouraged us to bring the show back.

I'm in my own little world right now, thinking about everything that's happened over the last few days. I gave Delilah the reins to be the head of the show and she's blabbering on and on about everything that we've experienced thus far. I see her mouth moving, but the words coming out of her mouth are reminiscent of the teachers on Charlie Brown. One thing, however, catches my attention.

"I also have some sad news to share with everyone listening," she says.

"I was taking a walk on the beach the other day, soaking in the beautiful weather when I stumbled across a dead body," she continues. Saying it seems to come naturally to her at this point and she keeps any shred of sadness out of her voice.

"Ugh," I chime in, "he wasn't my favorite person in the world, but I'd never have wished that on him."

"Detective Carpenter was on the Knock Knock Killer case in Milan eight months ago. He tried to help us, but—"

"Not to speak ill of the dead, but he didn't do shit," I say with my newfound arrogance.

"He really did leave you two out to dry," Riley says.

I look back over to Paul and Remi. Remi is fully engrossed in our conversation, but Paul looks annoyed. Looking up at us, then back down to his phone, then back up at us. It makes me suspicious, but then again, most things do these days after what we've been through. He makes eye contact with me and gives me another wide grin, flashing another thumbs up my way.

As we continue our conversation, the hairs on the back of my neck begin to stand on end, and I'm not sure why. Maybe it's because the last time we were in the studio talking about the Knock Knock Killer, I watched a girl get her brains blown out by the girl I'm engaged to. The memory of that moment is permanently burned into my brain.

My thoughts are jumping from one thing to the next, from replaying that night in my head to the current predicament we find ourselves in. We have nothing on this killer just like we didn't have anything on Tom in the beginning. We never really did procure new evidence, but he and Tatum randomly decided to make themselves known, trying to take everything from me just as everything was ripped from him at a young age.

We are about to wrap up the first episode of the new show when I realize all three of us broke the golden rule of recording a podcast: shutting off our ringers on our phones. All three of our phones start chiming and ringing incessantly. We all dig into our pockets quickly trying to silence them, but the chiming won't stop. Text message after text message comes through one right after the other and we all finally get them to quiet down.

Before looking at the screen, I glance at Paul and Remi and Remi has a slight look of annoyance on his face. He's going to have to edit it out, but Paul, on the other hand, is smiling widely. I know what he's hoping for: he wants it to be the killer. That would send our ratings sky high. We all look down at our phones and check what the messages were as our phones are still vibrating in our hands. It all seems like a garbled mess of random thoughts and I notice that the three of us are in a group chat with one unknown number, which is the one texting in.

"Before we end this episode," I say into the microphone, "everyone listening out there probably heard all of the phones going off. I want you to know this wasn't staged. This is very real and I'm going to read all of the messages the three of us just received."

I take a deep breath then begin to read the messages: "Cooper, Delilah and Riley," that's all that the first one says, followed by, "Come to Milan, follow my orders or watch your families die live on YouTube." I'm reading all of these into the microphone.

The threats continue in a non-stop barrage of harassment and taunting. A fleeting thought runs through my mind that maybe we *should* go back to Milan. Maybe we should do what they say, then kill them. We've done it before, I'm sure we could take down someone who thinks they can pull off what Tom did. Then another text pops through and I read it, then hesitate to say it out loud. I look up at Delilah, who I can see has tears welling up in her eyes. She looks up to make eye contact with me and, without speaking, I see the permission she is giving me to say it.

"LOL," it starts, "except orphan Delilah."

The tears begin to run down her cheeks as I say the words out loud. I know the text didn't come from me, from my mind, but I hate that I hurt her that way for the sake of entertainment. She gives me a look of understanding and I know everything is going to be okay.

Riley and I exchange a glance, too, and I can almost read his mind and know what he is thinking, but I don't know why. I can see in his eyes that he wants to return to Ohio. But why? When he didn't want to be involved before, why is he so eager to help this time around?

"Based on the mood in the studio right now, I think this will be the end of this week's episode of the return of the *Knock Knock Podcast*," I say into the microphone solemnly.

"Tune in next week and hopefully we will have more information to share with you."

Remi cuts the recording and gives us the all clear. The three of us remain silent for a bit, then Paul busts down the door into the studio with his typical managerial spirit.

"That was fucking incredible," he shouts, "who would have thought you three would have gotten a text from the killer in the middle of recording!"

I want to be angry with him, hell, I want to haul off and punch him right in his stupid face, but I know he's just doing his job. It's his responsibility to make sure the show continues and that we don't quit.

"You two," he starts, with energy flowing through his words, "three, I mean, this is fucking incredible. The ratings are going to be huge and that's just the beginning. Are you all going to go to Milan?"

He continues as though he's already made the decision for us to go back to Ohio. The only thing on his mind are the ratings and the money. He's just rambling on and on about how good it would be for the show, how great it would be for the listeners, how amazing it would be for us.

"We aren't going," I say firmly, interrupting him as he continues to blather on and on.

"What do you mean?" he asks with true confusion on his face.

"I mean we aren't going to Ohio and you *can't* make us," I say, figuratively putting my foot down.

Paul saunters toward me and has a look on his face that I hadn't seen up to this point. Slowly, he gets up to me and we are almost nose to nose and with his index finger, he pokes me in the shoulder.

"You," he starts, "will do whatever the hell I tell you to do." He says it almost threateningly, and although he doesn't come out and say it, it feels like there's an "or else" at the end of that sentence.

"No," I say, pushing him as he turns around to walk away, "I won't do anything that will put any of us at risk. Do you understand me?"

He turns back around then says, "Mark my words, if you refuse to do what I say, I will end you."

He turns around again and slams the door on his way out. The walls of the studio shake with the force and the silence in the room is deadly quiet. The three of us just look at one another, then from behind me I hear a voice chime in, forgetting Remi was there and just witnessed the spat between us.

"G…good work today guys. Solid episode. I'll get it cut and uploaded for you," Remi says timidly.

"Thanks, Remi," I say, and without another word, I walk out of the studio with Delilah and Riley following behind me.

We step out and I can see Paul walking down the other end of the hall. There is a fire growing in the pit of my stomach and I'm sure if I had my pistol on me, I'd have fired one right into the back of his head, so thankfully I don't have it. My anger has been off the charts lately.

"What the hell was that?" Delilah asks.

"I'm not sure," I reply.

CHAPTER THIRTY-FIVE

DELILAH CARNEY

We all head back to the house, driving in silence for the most part until I can't keep quiet; I've got to know what that was about. I break the silence and turn to make sure I can see both Cooper and Riley.

"What the hell was that back there?" I ask.

"I'm not sure," Cooper answers.

"I'm not either," Riley says.

"What do you think he was up to?" I ask.

"I mean, he's always trying to stir shit up," Cooper says, "but I don't know what that was, that was different."

"Meanwhile, I have no clue what the fuck is going on," says Riley, "but the dude is kind of a dick."

"What do you think he meant when he said he'd end you?" I ask.

Cooper shakes his head in disbelief. Paul has always been a pretty nice guy to us and a hell of a show manager. The three of us get along fine and I think Cooper is even a little bit intimidated by him, though he doesn't want to show it. Despite the difference in their status, Cooper respects him for some reason, and that's cool because that's how it should be.

"I have no idea," he answers in a tone that suggests everything is going to be fine.

I'm not convinced at all and I've got to say that I'm completely fucking terrified. I have no idea what is going on, but something tells me that Paul was telling the truth. I can see it in Cooper's eyes and I know he's scared too, but he's trying not to show it. I can see it. I can feel it.

"Maybe he has some intel that we don't," I suggest.

"Maybe," says Cooper, "but we're going to have to ask him at some point."

I don't respond, but Cooper's right. We're going to have to find out what the deal is eventually and if he *does* have information, why wouldn't he share it with us?

Entertainment value, I think. It's all about entertainment value for the show to him and it's more exciting when we find clues by ourselves.

'Hopefully, whatever it is, it'll be good news," says Riley.

"I mean, that's what I'm hoping for," says Cooper. I can see him biting his lip as he drives down the road.

Cooper never gets into arguments, so to have him do anything with Paul was fucking scary. I mean, Cooper is normally really polite and non-confrontational, but now I can't help but wonder what was up. I've got to say, I'm feeling a bit taken back by him. I'm not mad at him or anything, because he is who he is and that's really cool, but it's just that he's always been so timid and I wonder what happened to him back there. I'm not sure, but I think he might be growing a pair. I mean, he's always trying to do the right thing and he's always been the guy who takes care of me, but despite all the shit we get into, I've always been the confident one.

I'm feeling a little shell shocked realizing something could possibly happen to us and that makes me fucking sick considering what's growing inside me right now. I don't even want to think about it, but I can't help it. It's all I've been thinking about, and it fucking sucks and it pisses me off because I wish I could do something, anything, to stop it.

Instinctively, I reach down and rub my stomach.

It's okay little one, I will do everything I can to keep you safe.

I catch Cooper side-eyeing me and I quickly remove my hands from my stomach. I can't tell him I'm pregnant—not yet at least.

CHAPTER THIRTY-SIX

COOPER COBB

As we pull into the driveway, I can tell Delilah is still on edge. I don't blame her. Paul's threat was not something to be taken lightly and it's clear that it's weighing on all of us. I want to reassure her, but I don't even know what to say. Instead, I focus on getting inside and getting some rest.

But as we walk through the door, I notice something odd. There's a faint smell in the air. It's a sickly sweet scent, like burnt sugar. My heart rate picks up as I realize what it is. Gasoline.

"Guys, do you smell that?" I ask, my eyes scanning the room for any sign of danger.

They both nod, looking equally worried.

"I'll check the house," Riley says, pulling out his knife.

Delilah and I follow him, looking around the living room for any sign of a break-in or an intruder. I proceed to run to the front hall closet where I keep my safe. I type in the code hastily and remove my gun, cocking it as I run back to their side.

"What the fuck is going on?" Delilah asks.

"Delilah, listen," I start, as I grab her by the waist. "I need you to get out of the house and call the police, tell them someone has broken into our house and it reeks of gasoline."

"But, I can't leave—" she starts.

"Go," I tell her before I look deeply into her eyes and plant a kiss on her lips.

She nods, getting on the phone with the police and relaying our situation as she runs out the front door. As she does, Riley and I make our way through the house and check the perimeter, looking for a break-in. Everything appears normal, except for the smell. It begins to smell stronger the closer we get to the living room.

"I think it's in the living room," I say, verifying my suspicions.

Riley nods, then says, "We need to get out of here. Something isn't right." I can see the fearful look on his face.

"You go, I'm going to investigate," I say.

"Cooper," he says, "I can't."

"Get the *fuck* out, Riley!" I yell at him.

Riley retreats toward the hall and out the front door as I look around the living room, but I still see no sign that anyone was here. It looks as we left it; nothing is thrown around, and with the exception of the gasoline smell, you'd think whoever was here couldn't find what they were looking for. Then it dawns on me and my eyes grow wide. Whoever this is wasn't here looking for anything. They came in, dumped gasoline all over the house, and left. I can see a soaking wet throw pillow on the sofa. I lean down to sniff it and instantly pull away. The aroma is so strong it makes me gag.

As the coughing and hacking subsides and I catch my breath, I look up and out the back window of our home and catch a glimpse of someone standing in the distance. It looks like they are holding a long steel pipe, using their shoulder to brace it. I squint my eyes to see if I can see them better, but to no avail. All I can see is a person in the distance wearing a black cloak with a black hood covering their face—similar to what Tom used to wear when he was stalking me.

My eyes widen even more as I realize what they are holding and I abruptly turn on my heels and run toward the front door. As I swing it open, in the distance, I hear a loud bang and then the sound of a projectile flying through the air. As I run out the front door, I see Delilah and Riley and I scream at them.

"Get down," I yell.

My feet suddenly give way beneath me and I'm blasted through the air like a discarded toy amidst an explosive array of fragmented wood. Before I fly away, I catch a glimpse of Delilah and Riley desperately throwing themselves to the ground. My flight seems to last forever, yet is over in the blink of an eye as I crash down hard onto the ground. The roaring sound of flames crackles menacingly behind me as sirens blare in the distance. Abruptly, my world fades to black.

CHAPTER THIRTY-SEVEN

COOPER COBB

I awake to the sound of steady beeping and the sterile scent of a hospital room. I attempt to open my eyes, but it feels like my eyelids are fighting me and keep trying to close. Still, I catch quick glimpses of the room around me. I try to sit up, but a sharp pain shoots through my spine and I collapse back onto the bed. My eyes dart around the room, taking in the beeping monitors and plastic tubes snaking in and out of my arm.

The memories flood back to me like a wave crashing onto shore. The explosion, Delilah, Riley. I try to call out to them, but my throat feels raw and scratchy. I look for the nurse call button, pressing it repeatedly until a nurse rushes in.

"How are you feeling?" she asks in a soft voice, checking my vitals.

"What happened to my friends? Are they okay?" I croak out, my voice barely audible.

"They're fine. They are in the cafeteria getting a bite to eat. They've barely left your side. I don't think I've seen them eat for three days."

"Three days?" I raspily yell out, "I've been here for three days?"

"Actually—" she starts, but is interrupted by Delilah.

"Oh my god, Cooper," she says through stifled sobs.

She sets her food tray down on the table at the foot of my bed and runs to my side, throwing herself over my body, which causes me to wince. My entire body aches and throbs, though I'm happy to see her again.

"Sorry," she says as she wipes tears from her eyes.

"It's okay," I assure her.

I'm barely aware of the throbbing in my body as she gently wraps her arms around me. All thoughts about the pain evaporate, replaced by a sense of warmth and security. She looks deeply into my eyes, then opens her mouth and begins to speak.

"Cee, I have something to tell you," she says.

"What is it?" I ask, with a smile.

"I'm—"

Just then, Riley bursts inside the room and interrupts her. The walls shake with the force from him throwing the door open and I can see my IV bag rock. The nurse turns and looks at Riley.

"This is a *hospital*, not an amusement park," she says with a scowl. She is completely over his shit, which tells me I've definitely been here longer than three days.

"Holy shit, man," he says, "did you have a good nap?"

He walks up to the end of my bed and stuffs his mouth with food quickly. It must have been a while since he ate considering the ferocity of which he shovels it in.

"So, how long *was* I out?" I ask.

Delilah and Riley exchange a glance as if they don't want to come clean and tell me, but I'm definitely suspicious that it's been way longer than three days now. Even the nurse looks at the two of them as she checks my IV drip. The three just stare at one another for what seems like an eternity as if they are having a telepathic discussion about who is going to tell me.

"Cee," Delilah says with her familiar, sweet tone, "you were in a coma for two weeks. Do you remember what happened? The doctors said you may have some memory issues."

My eyes snap shut and an orange blast detonates in my head. I relive the explosion, feeling myself flying through the air as shards of wood slice through me like bullets. I glimpse the sky a few times before being engulfed by darkness, grateful that I can't recall the moment of impact.

"Rocket launcher," I whisper as my eyes pop open.

"W…what?" Delilah asks.

"Rocket launcher," I say again, louder this time.

"What do you mean, 'rocket launcher'?"

I look around the room, scanning for any potential threat. My heart races as I try to make sense of what I just vividly remembered.

"I remember a rocket launcher. It was aimed at us," I explain to Delilah. Her eyes widen in fear.

"What are we going to do?" she asks, almost in a panic.

"What can I do from here?" I ask, my voice shaking. I can't shake the feeling of unease, knowing I can't do anything from this bed.

"We need to leave," I say to Delilah as I start to swing my legs to my right and out of the bed, but I am quickly stopped by the nurse.

"No, Mr. Cobb, you can't go anywhere," she says.

"Alright, let's do this," says Riley, egging me on.

"Cooper, you were just in a coma for two weeks, you need to rest," says Delilah, helping the nurse try to coax me back into bed.

"I've rested long enough. You can't hold me against my will," I say to the nurse, pointing a finger at her as though she is a small child who just did something wrong.

The nurse backs away and Delilah looks at her expectantly like she's hoping she comes up with some idea to keep me here.

"Cee," she says, looking back at me,"you need to recover."

"As long as I am in this bed, stuck in this room, more people are going to die, the people in this hospital are not safe. No one is safe around me. Not you, not Riley, no one. Let me go," I say firmly.

She looks down at the bed, avoiding eye contact with me. Something's up—something she doesn't want to tell me, but I need to know.

"What?" I ask her, but she just looks up, still avoiding me and looking toward Riley.

"More people have died," he says.

"H...how many?" I ask.

He lets out a long, heavy sigh and averts his gaze. His lips press into a thin line and he runs a hand through his hair, avoiding my eyes. I can feel the tension in the air as he struggles between wanting to help and not wanting to give me the answer.

"Tell me," I demand.

He sighs again, then looks up at me. "Thirty-two," he says.

Terror races through my veins and I feel like my chest might burst. My vision blurs in horror and my stomach churns and twists in agony. The pounding in my head is deafening as if it will shatter my skull, and the frantic rhythm of my heart thunders so loud that I think it might be heard for miles. My thoughts are a tangled web of nonsense and I'm trying to form words, though nothing comes out of my mouth.

"The house," I finally say, "what about the house?"

"It's okay," says Delilah, "it's gone, and we are staying in a hotel for now. The insurance company is paying for it. We've got this all figured out. You don't need to worry about it."

I know Delilah is trying to make sure that I don't stress. I'm sure the doctors have told her to make sure that if and when I wake up, to try not to add stress to my life, which is impossible these days. I look away from the two and everyone in the room stays silent. I look to the nurse who is now keeping an extremely close eye on me.

"I need to speak to the doctor now. I need to get out of here," I say.

The nurse turns on her heels and exits the room. I look at Delilah and Riley who are both staring at each other. I know they're thinking I'm crazy. I'm starting to think maybe I'm insane, too. Who wakes up from a coma and immediately tries to leave? How many other people have a copycat serial killer after them?

Not many, I'm sure. The doctor quickly enters the room and tries to introduce himself, but I cut him off.

"When can I leave?" I ask immediately.

"You need a few days of rest, Cooper," he says, "we can't have you waking up from a coma and walking right out of here. There can be many complications and side effects of a coma," he says.

"Walk me through all the potential side effects and *I* will determine if I'm well enough to leave. As I told her," I gesture to the nurse who is now standing in the doorway to my room, "you can't hold me against my will."

"The less severe risks of being in a coma would be a urinary tract infection and blood clots in the legs, sometimes bedsores," he begins.

My back end doesn't feel sore, so I think I'm good there, but all of these people are starting to become a *big* pain in my ass.

"The worst of it would be brain damage," the doctor says.

"Well shit, we know his brain is damaged," Riley chimes in. I immediately flip him the bird.

"Love you, too, buddy," he says sarcastically.

"What do we need to do to make sure I don't have any lasting effects from this prolonged nap?" I ask.

"We will need to run some tests and make sure there are no blood clots, probably do a CT scan and an MRI. That should tell us everything we need to know."

"Do the tests," I demand.

"They can take a couple days to get you scheduled and in for," he says, diminishing any hope I have of getting out of this godforsaken hospital today.

"Do the tests today or I get up and walk out of here with my ass hanging out of the back end of this gown, mooning you the whole way down the hallway." I threaten, albeit, it's not much of a threat.

"Very well," he says, "I'll see what I can do."

As the doctor walks out of the room, the nurse trails behind him. I can sense their annoyance with me at this point, but it doesn't matter. All that matters is finding and taking down the killer who has been preying on innocent people. I need to leave this hospital room and get back to work as soon as possible.

CHAPTER THIRTY-EIGHT

COOPER COBB

The tests take longer than I anticipated, but I finally receive the all-clear from the doctors. My head is still pounding, but I refuse to let that stop me from continuing the search for the killer. I grab my jacket and the three of us head out to the car, ready to hit the streets once again. As we drive through the small town, I can't shake the feeling that we are being watched. It's a familiar feeling, one that I've experienced many times in the last year. I glance around, but I can't see anyone suspicious.

We pull up to a red light and stop. Another car pulls up next to us and I immediately recognize the man behind the steering wheel. It's someone I haven't seen in a couple weeks, ever since the blow up at the recording studio. I roll down my window and wave to get his attention, and he glances over with an almost sinister smile on his face. It seems to click in his head who is trying to get his attention and he rolls down the window.

"Cooper, buddy. How are you?" Paul says.

"Other than a headache and a concussion, I'm doing pretty well," I say.

I keep my brows furrowed. After our last encounter, I'm suspicious of him and I don't want him to think that everything is okay now. My memory is completely intact and I definitely remember how much of a dick he was in the studio that day.

"Listen, dude, I wanted to say I'm sorry for how I reacted that day. That was wrong of me," he says as he glances up at the light, ensuring it's staying red.

I pause, considering his words. He looks genuine enough, but I've been burned before. I narrow my eyes at him and ask, "Why the sudden change of heart?"

He sighs heavily, running a hand through his hair. "Look, I've been going through some stuff lately. Personal stuff. And I took it out on you. It wasn't fair and I'm truly sorry."

I study him for a moment longer before finally relenting. "Okay. Apology accepted."

He visibly relaxes and a small smile tugs at the corner of his lips. "Thank you. I really appreciate it." We lapse into silence for a moment before he speaks up again. "Hey, let's grab a coffee sometime." I hesitantly agree, unsure if I trust him completely yet.

"That sounds nice," I say, "we'll make it a plan when I'm feeling a little better. With that being said, I need some time off to recover. We aren't going to be able to record any more episodes for a while."

"Totally understand," he says, and he sounds sincere, which is shocking to me that the guy who only cares about money is being understanding about this. My head continues to pound and the sunlight shining on me isn't helping matters any. This feels like the worst migraine I've had in my life.

"Thanks, Paul, I really appreciate it. I'll keep you updated on my recovery. I'm sure I'll be ready in a couple of weeks."

"Sure," he says graciously as he puts his sunglasses back on his face, "see you then."

The light turns green and with an animalistic roar, he slams his foot hard onto the gas pedal, pushing the Lexus LS 500 to take off like a shot. The engine's throaty howl pierces through the air as it strains under the violent acceleration.

"Well, that was nice," says Riley.

Delilah turns to me, her face practically saying what's on our minds: that Paul's apology felt insincere. I know Paul too well; he always has a hidden agenda and that agenda usually leads back to money. The churning in my stomach returns suddenly and I look at Delilah with a fearful look in my eyes.

"Pull over," I say, struggling to get the words out.

I swing the passenger side door open and just as I tilt my head toward the ground, I begin to dry heave with nothing but small amounts of bile dripping to the earth beneath me. I forgot that I hadn't eaten so there was nothing to actually come out. I grab a napkin from the glove compartment, wipe my mouth off, and turn to Delilah, who has a horrified look on her face.

"Probably just the concussion, I'll be fine," I assure her.

I can't help but feel unsettled when I hear Paul's name. My body trembles with fear at the thought of what he could be plotting, and yet, despite everything, some part of me tells me that he couldn't possibly be responsible for the murders. Still, something about him is off—I just can't put my finger on it. Is he a killer? No. But is his behavior suspicious? Absolutely.

CHAPTER THIRTY-NINE

DELILAH CARNEY

I watch as Cooper struggles to regain his composure, his body trembling with concern. I can see the conflict playing out in his mind, and I know that he's just as scared as I am. The fact that Paul might be involved in the murders is an unsettling thought, but I can't ignore the feeling that something isn't right about him. Ever since he entered our lives, there has been this sense of unease that has lingered in the background, but Cooper is probably right. Paul might not be involved in the murders, but he's definitely up to something; the dude is an asshole, but definitely not a killer.

But what can we do? We can't just accuse Paul of being a killer without any evidence. And yet, the more I think about it, the more I realize that we can't afford to ignore the possibility. We need to find out what Paul's motives are, and whether he's involved in the murders. As we continue driving, I can feel the tension between us growing. We're all lost in our own thoughts, trying to make sense of everything that has happened.

The silence in the car is deafening while we drive down the road back to the hotel. I can sense Riley's unease, and it's making me anxious as well. I decide to break the ice.

"You holding up okay, Riley?"

He glances at me in the rearview mirror and nods with a forced smile. "Yeah, just trying to process everything and prepare for what's next."

I nod in understanding. "I know it's a lot to take in. But hey, we're in this together. We'll figure it out."

I see Riley visibly relax at my words. "Thanks, Delilah. I appreciate that."

We drive on in silence for a while longer until we reach our destination: a nice little hotel on the outskirts of town. All three of us get out of the car and none of us speak; even Cooper, who always has something to say, is staying quiet, but that could just be because he's not feeling well.

We walk down the hall to our rooms. The insurance company was cool enough to provide us with two rooms so the three of us weren't sharing; a very out of the norm response from an insurance company, but most everyone in the country knows our story, so I just had to turn on the waterworks on the phone with them and *voilà*, two rooms.

When we reach the doors, Riley and I turn to look at one another while Cooper, getting more impatient by the second, waits for me to unlock the door.

"It's going to be okay Riles," I say, "I promise."

"I know," he replies.

I insert the key card into the slot and open the door, holding it for Cooper while he enters. I begin to enter myself, but Riley stops me.

"Delilah, promise me something," he says.

"What's that?"

"Promise me you're not involved this time."

The thought makes me laugh and I wrap my arms around myself as if to hold in the laughter. The sound bounces off the walls of the hotel hallway, echoing until my laughter dies. My hand covers my mouth and I can still taste the flavor of humor on my tongue, but Riley just stares at me deadpan.

"I'm not. I can't be. I'm still too traumatized by everything we went through. You know what the last image is that I see in my mind every night before I go to sleep?"

Riley looks at me, confused. I'm sure part of it is inquisitive and part of it is simply confusion because I've never opened up to him like this before.

"I see the blood splattering from Tatum's head, painting the wall like an angry artist creating a new piece of abstract art. The trauma from that alone. I just want it to be over, but I have a feeling it'll never be over."

I begin to walk into the room again, hoping to put an end to this conversation, but Riley stops me one more time.

"Delilah, one more thing. I'm going to do everything I can to keep you safe."

Now I'm the one looking at him with a puzzled look on my face.

"Have you told him yet?" he asks in a hushed tone while pointing to his own belly.

"How did you—"

"Just a feeling. Tell him soon. He needs to know."

In a flash, Riley slips into his bedroom and I'm left standing in the hallway with my hand still on the door handle with confusion etched across my face. I step into the room and close the door.

CHAPTER FORTY

DELILAH CARNEY

Lying in the silence of our hotel room, I replay the decision over and over in my mind. It feels like such a monumental moment that I am scared to reveal it, yet at the same time, I know it would make him so happy. Cooper stirs behind me, his arm softly enveloping me in a hug. This is exactly where I want to be: with him. But why did it take me so long to see that this was who I needed all along?

I wiggle closer to him and the warmth of his embrace is slowly lulling me to sleep. I'm struggling to keep my eyes open and every time my eyelids fall, I pop them back open quickly. I've decided: I'm going to tell him. I want—no, I need—to tell him that I am carrying his child. I roll over and face him, and as soon as I do, he gives me that loving smile, that smile that says so many words without him having to speak a single syllable, and he gives me a quick peck on the nose. I smile back and my vision goes blurry again. I can't keep my eyes open, and now, I don't think I want to. What I want is to fall asleep in his arms and feel, for just a bit, that everything is okay.

"I love you, Dee," his voice is echoing in my head as reality fades and I'm met with immense darkness.

***

I feel my body slowly drift into an unfamiliar place, and then I experience a sudden impact as I crash down onto the even ground. Gently, I open my eyes and see that a small patch of grass is caressing my legs. Taking in this moment of solace, I feel a wave of calmness wash over me while my breathing slows. As the darkness begins to lift, I look up to meet an enchanting full moon hanging in the night sky, bathing everything in a gentle lunar light.

I slowly lift myself back onto my feet, pushing on the ground with my hands. As I get up, I wipe the dirt off of myself while I look around, trying to figure out the unfamiliar, yet familiar landscape.

I've been here before, I think.

I begin to walk around, trying to find my way out, when I suddenly find myself falling to the ground again after kicking something solid and losing my footing. I roll over onto my back and stare up at the stars and I spot a couple of constellations; I can see the big and little dipper. I've never taken a moment to *really* stare up at the stars, but it's a gentle reminder of how small and insignificant we are in our universe.

I look to my feet and I can see what I tripped on: it looks like a large rock. I dig into my pocket for my phone and turn on the flashlight, trying to get a better look at the object. As I come to the realization of what it is, I can hear a faint screaming coming from behind me. It sounds like someone is in trouble. It's a female voice.

I scramble to my feet and start running. I don't know what I'm running toward, and no matter how much I have second thoughts and my brain tells my feet to stop running, I can't. It feels like I've lost total autonomy over my own body and my legs just want to keep going. I run through the woods, dodging more and more of the solid objects, and I start to notice names on them—names that I recognize.

Roberts, Prescott, Carney, until I reach the last one in a long row of headstones. I've been transported back to the cemetery where we ended Tom's reign of terror all those months ago. The last headstone reads Langford. It's Tom's headstone.

Why is he buried in the same place as his victims?

The screaming is getting louder and louder with every step I take, but I can't see the person who is making the sound. It's echoing all around me, bouncing off of the trees and the headstones and reverberating. It almost sounds like someone is yelling into a microphone with the reverb turned all the way up. I'm running so fast, it feels like my feet are about to lift off and I'm going to go airborne. I dodge around a tree and that's when I spot her.

There's a young woman standing in the middle of the cemetery. I quickly hide behind another tree and peek around the trunk. I can see her sitting on the ground tied up with a heavy-looking rope and a piece of fabric around her neck. She is screaming for help over and over again. I inspect her surroundings and it looks like she's alone, so I dart out from behind the tree and run up to her.

She's about my age with brunette hair and she seems unharmed until she looks up at me. There is blood running out of her eye sockets and only the whites of her eyes are showing. She stops screaming and stares at me for a moment as if she can see me, but I'm pretty sure she's blind. She points behind me.

"Help me," she says.

Terror consumes me as I feel a presence looming behind me. I whirl around to see a massive, faceless figure hurtling towards me, and with one vicious shove, I'm thrown to the ground. Every muscle is tense, and my screams fill up the air, but no one seems to hear them. Desperation washes over me like an icy wave as I scramble for escape. A thunderous banging interrupts my panicked thoughts—someone's pounding on a door, but it feels too late for rescue. Tears blur my vision as I realize this might be the end of my journey.

***

My whole body twitches hard, like when you're having a dream that you're falling. I can feel wetness running down my face —sweat dripping down onto my pillow. My breathing is heavy and I feel dizzy, but one thing from the nightmare remains: the pounding on our hotel door. Cooper stirs awake also, much slower and more peacefully than I did.

"What the fuck is that?" he asks as he sleepily pulls himself out of bed and stumbles to the door. He looks through the peephole.

"Riley, what the—" he starts as he begins pulling the door open, but Riley bursts into the room, shoving the door open as he runs in.

"Dude, what the hell?" Cooper says.

"He…has…Alicia," he manages to strain out through breaths.

"Who is Alicia?" I ask as I sit up in bed. Riley almost knocking the door off its hinges was almost enough for me to forget my nightmare.

"I'll tell you on the way," he says, "but we have to go back to Milan."

The three of us stare at one another in stunned silence.

CHAPTER FORTY-ONE

RILEY STEVENS

Lying in bed—my happy place. I need to decompress; this is all so intense. All I can do is stand back and watch it all happen. Cooper, the explosion, the fight at the studio. I feel so helpless. I feel like I can't help my best friends. Why am I even still here? I should go home. I should leave. I feel like I'm more of a hindrance than anything else. Maybe it was just the awkwardness of the whole ordeal.

I remember a couple of weeks ago when the fight happened in the studio. I've never seen Cooper get so angry or stand his ground like that. He's been more of a go-with-the-flow, do-as-I'm-told type of person. I think everything that's gone down in the last few months has changed him. He's still my best friend and I'll never leave his side, but the look in his eyes did terrify me.

It was a look you would expect a born-killer to give their latest victim right before plunging a knife into their heart. It's the look I imagine you give someone before wrapping your hands around their neck and squeezing until they stop breathing. If looks could kill, Paul would have been dead, but then Cooper almost was.

I take a deep breath, exhale slowly, and stare at the ceiling wondering how I got myself into this mess. How did all of this start as I was getting off the plane to visit my best friends? I wanted nothing more than a fun, peaceful couple of weeks to hang out and enjoy their company. It feels as though this was planned perfectly by someone, though I know my decisions and my actions brought me here, and now I'm involved and there's no way out.

On top of that, I can't just leave them; that would be a shitty thing to do to the two that I call my closest friends. I'd distanced myself from them once and it made me feel like a steaming pile of human garbage to do it, although every time Cooper needed me, I was there as fast as I could be. With every wild theory he had, with every helping hand he needed, I was there, and when it mattered the most, I couldn't sit idly by and watch everything unfold without being there for him. I knew he needed my assistance and every single day I live with the fear of what might have happened had I decided to be a pussy and sit back and watch.

Now I lie here and wonder what Cooper is thinking about doing. I know where his heart is. I know what he wants to do, but will he decide we need to return to our hometown and face down yet another killer?

God, please don't, I think.

I can hear muffled sounds through the wall, but I can't tell if they're talking or what else might be going on in there. I hope Delilah told him about the baby; that might make him choose differently, though it seems we aren't safe whether we stay in Lexington or go back to Milan. It sounds like Delilah is screaming, but I can't hear Cooper. *Maybe it's good screaming?* I laugh to myself.

The room beside me illuminates briefly and I look over toward my phone. I grab my phone and look. It's Alicia texting me, asking if I'm awake. A smile flashes across my face as I read her words. She makes me the happiest I've been in forever.

I click into her message and click the phone button to give her a call. The line rings and I remember, with everything going on, I still haven't told Delilah or even Cooper about her. Not important right now, though I know they'd still be happy for me. After about two rings, she answers.

"Hey, Riley," she says, her sweet voice ringing through my head.

"Hey, babe," I say, "what's up?"

"I think I might be in danger," she says, her voice shaking and timid.

"What do you mean? Where's your dad?"

"I saw someone lurking outside of the house. He's not home, I don't know where he is," she says, her voice trembling more with each word.

"Okay, stay on the phone with me."

I run over to the door and grab the handle. I'm not sure what I'm going to do, being almost three and a half hours away, but the only thing I can think of is that I need to alert Cooper and Delilah and we need to get in the car and go *now*. The phone line is now completely silent and I'm hesitating to ask if she's still on the line when suddenly I hear a crash and a loud bang on the other line, then Alicia screams at the top of her lungs.

"Riley, help!" she shouts, then the line goes dead.

My heart races at the sound of her scream, and I know I have to act fast. As I run to Cooper and Delilah's room, all I can hear is her scream echoing in my head. I reach their room and pound on the door as hard and fast as I can. I look up and down the hall, making sure no one is peeking out to get a look at the psychotic freak pounding on a seemingly random hotel room door. Tears are streaming down my face as I continue to slam my fists on the barrier between us.

Come on guys.

Cooper finally opens the door, and before he can even get it open an inch, I find myself standing in their room. I see the confused looks on their faces and I need to tell them, but the mixture of fear and anxiety coursing through my veins is making it difficult to catch my breath. My heart is pounding out of my chest as I attempt to get the words out.

"Dude, what the hell?" Cooper says with a slightly annoyed edge to his voice.

"He…has…Alicia," I finally manage to say through my breaths.

"Who is Alicia?" Delilah asks. I'd almost forgotten I still hadn't told them about her yet.

"I'll tell you on the way," I say, finally catching my breath, "but we have to go back to Milan."

The three of us stare at each other for what feels like an eternity; truthfully, I don't know how much time is passing. Seconds feel like minutes and minutes feel like hours. All I know is, for every single moment we continue to stand in this hotel room, Alicia could be hurt, or worse, dead.

"Let's go," I scream at them. I've never taken a tone like that with Cooper and I can see in his eyes that he's ready to grab his keys and run out the door, but there's also hesitation in his posture.

"I'm going with or without you," I say defiantly, "come with me or not, I'll be the one to take down the Knock Knock Killer this time."

I know I can't take him down on my own, I know I need their help, but a little bit of confidence will convince them to pack up and leave, not that it would take much. Most of our belongings were consumed by the fire at the house.

"Grab your things," Cooper says as he turns and looks at Delilah, "we need to go back to Milan."

PART 5

CHAPTER FORTY-TWO

COOPER COBB

Driving back to Milan feels like an eternity, and I can barely contain my fear and anger as I picture Alicia, a girl I've never met, alone and terrified. Riley goes on and on for the entire ride about her; how great she is, how in love he is, how beautiful she is, and how we would love her if we met her. His vivid description of her makes me feel like I do know her already, but I don't know anyone named Alicia. The picture he paints of her feels familiar to me, though, but I think I'm just relating to my best friend.

We enter the Milan city limits and when we finally arrive outside her house, Riley jumps out of the car before I even have the chance to park. We didn't bother calling the cops; we know the Milan police department is useless.

"Alicia!" he shouts and bangs on the door with such force that I think it might crack. When there is no answer, my heart begins to race. Cautiously, I reach out and test the handle—the door opens easily. As I step into the darkness of the unknown, a dread creeps over me. This house is familiar to me, too familiar. The layout is like a nightmare from my past. My brain screams for me to turn around and run back, but I push forward despite the fear paralyzing my body. In the distance, I can hear Delilah and Riley's footsteps from another room.

"Guys," I yell, and almost immediately they come running to my side.

"What is it, Cee?" Delilah asks, wrapping her arm around mine.

"I know this house," I say, confidently.

"What do you mean?" Riley asks.

My legs march forward, my heart pounding in my chest as I glare at Riley. His beady eyes dart around and he stumbles back in fear, sweat dripping from his brow. He's powerless to stop me as I raise my fist, ready to unleash a fury upon him. But before I can land the blow, Delilah steps in front of him, unafraid and determined to shield him from any harm that might come his way. I'm ensnared in an invisible prison of my own doing and it's all I can do to stand there, shaking with rage.

"Cooper, what are you doing?" she yells.

"Do you know whose house this is, Riles? Do you?" With every word, my volume increases.

"I don't know! Alicia and her dad just moved in a few months ago!" he yells, using his arms to shield himself from my impending punch.

"And let me guess," I say, running away from him and up the stairs directly in the foyer, "this is her bedroom, I'm assuming?"

"H…how do you know that?" he asks as he clambers back to his feet, cautiously moving toward the stairs as if I am about to leap the entire flight and tackle him. Delilah stays back and keeps her distance.

"This isn't…" Delilah starts, but I give her a look and she looks down at the ground, knowing her guess is the truth.

Riley looks back at Delilah, then to me, then to Delilah again.

"Alright, I'm lost," he says as Delilah looks back up at him with a defeated look on her face.

"It's Tatum's house," she says to him.

I push the bedroom door open, and it's like she never left. I know that she did, though. She left on a gurney with her brain matter splattered against the studio walls. As soon as I enter the room, the scent of lavender and vanilla drifts to me and wraps around my senses like a soft knit scarf. It is not burned into the atmosphere by candle wax or air fresheners; rather, it seems to have saturated itself right into the molecules of the room.

It's like she's still here, I think.

CHAPTER FORTY-THREE

COOPER COBB

It's hard to believe I'm back here, sitting in the same booth we used to sit in. My hands slide across the glossy wood as though it were yesterday. It almost feels like those hours have melted into one. The Milan Coffee Station was where the podcast came to life. Here, we shared some of our best ideas. Here, we developed episodes and pored over evidence for hours. Sometimes we just sat with our coffee and enjoyed each other's company.

The comforting smell of coffee grounds fills my nostrils as I stare anxiously into the depths of my cup. As the steam rises, contorting and transforming its form in the air, a wave of conflicting emotions washes over me. On one hand, I find solace in familiar warmth; on the other, I can't help but ponder what our lives would have been like had we never started our podcast. A fear lurks within me of Tom's ever-present revengeful nature and whether he would have come after us if it weren't for the show, although it seemed his motives were more personal.

I don't know what to do. Delilah and Riley are here, yet I feel so alone. I want to tell them to leave and get as far away from the Midwest as possible, maybe even to go east or west. But what if that isn't safe? What if they can't escape the mess that I created? The mess that my family started? Would it be selfish of me to try and finish it all by myself? I just don't know.

Delilah takes my arm, and it feels like a complete circle. The moment she touches my skin, I feel the rush of love throw itself onto me. It becomes everything. Every problem vanishes, every worry disappears; all that's left is the two of us. I look up and look into her eyes, and she gives me a little smirk and I can see in them that she will always have my back.

"What do we do now?" Delilah asks.

Riley stares up at me, the intensity of his gaze searing. As if I'm not already feeling an enormous amount of pressure, his eyes connect with mine and I can feel my heart racing in my chest. A wave of nausea floods over me as I realize that it is all on me to make this situation right; although, we've already learned from previous experiences that pushing boundaries too far will only bring out the beast in people.

With a deep breath, I simply lift my coffee cup to my lips and take a sip. I can feel the warmth of the beverage running all the way down my esophagus to my stomach. I set the cup down and look at the two of them as they stare at me expectantly.

"We poke the bear," I say confidently, "then we wait."

CHAPTER FORTY-FOUR

DELILAH CARNEY

I know what his intentions are, and I know they are good. I know he wants to defeat this evil and move on with our lives, but I can't help feeling that something bad is coming—something dangerous. It all feels similar, yet different than it did the last time. It feels more sinister, and it feels like something worse will hit us when we least expect it.

Cooper and Riley are still at the Milan Coffee Station concocting some sort of plan; God knows what it will be, but I decided to find a hotel and hunker down for the night. I'm not feeling as great as I could and I know it's the pregnancy. I reach down and rub my belly. I can feel a slight bulge, I think. Maybe not. I can't be more than six weeks along, eight at the most. There's no way I'm showing yet. I think it's just paranoia. Does Cooper know already and hasn't said anything to me? I hope so. It would make this easier; then I wouldn't have to tell him.

"Mama will keep you safe, little one," I say out loud to seemingly no one.

Can this little thing hear me yet? I don't know how any of this works. I'm terrified, nervous, and excited all at the same time and I know these feelings are normal. A part of me is also hoping it doesn't make it. It's morbid, I know, but in our little world, we have seen and are currently seeing more horror than most people see in their entire lives. Why would I want to bring a child into a world that is so unphased by physical violence against other humans? I think about myself even, this whole situation has made me apathetic. I feel nothing. Maybe it's trauma, but I have no emotion toward most of what's happening.

My phone vibrates next to me and causes me to jump from the unexpected notification. I reach for it, horrified at what I'm about to find on the screen.

How are you, sweetie?

It's Cooper's mom. She's always been so sweet, and when my family died, she took me in as if I was one of her own. She didn't have to do it, but she did, and I thank her every day for her generosity and love. I often wonder why she decided to give up Tom. I'll never say it to Cooper, but she's the root of all of this, though I know he recognizes it, too.

I think I know what Cooper is going to decide to do, and I think it's going to feel familiar to us. I think he's going to go for a dramatic climax to this part of our story. I think we are going to end up back in the studio taunting the killer the way we did before. The only problem is, what are they going to do in return? Who will be their victim? I can only assume everything will come to a head similarly to how it did the last time.

I hope I'm wrong, I hope it doesn't. I can't stomach having to shoot another person again. I knew it needed to happen before. I knew if I didn't make a move, Cooper wouldn't be with me today. I knew he was a goner, because I knew the plan. Make Cooper watch his parents die, then he dies. That was Tom's plan—he wanted to hurt Cooper in the most extreme way he possibly could in his final minutes, but my plan was different. I went along with it. I knew I needed to keep him safe so I agreed to everything Tom said. I tried to steer Cooper in the direction he needed to find out who was behind it without letting on that I was involved, though I never got my hands dirty. I didn't kill a single person besides Tatum, and that was to keep him safe.

I grab on to my stomach again and I'm not sure why. I need to keep this being inside me safe, but how do I do that? I get the feeling I'm going to have a larger part to play this time around in taking down whoever is doing this.

I feel for Riley, too. I've not met Alicia yet, let alone just finding out about her a few hours ago.

Who is this girl? I find myself repeating in my head. I close my eyes for a moment and I can instantly feel my entire body relax and can feel the swimmy feeling in my head, that sensation where you're aware of what's going on around you, but also know that sleep is imminent.

***

Suddenly I'm standing in the darkness with nothing around me. Just pitch black, as though I've been transported to the deepest darkest part of space, but there are no stars around me. No light for miles, except for right in front of me. A single building stands, with glass windows all along the facade. I squint my eyes as if that's going to help me see better, and it somewhat does. I recognize the building, but why can't I place it?

I urge my legs to begin moving forward toward the building, but it's a struggle. It feels like I'm trudging through thick muck and every step is difficult to make. It's as if my legs have concrete weights tied to them, but slowly and surely, I make my way closer to the building until I'm right in front of the windows.

I place my face against the glass and look inside. It's the Milan Coffee Station and there is no one around except for a couple of guys in a back corner booth who I recognize as Cooper and Riley. Cooper's got his thinking face on; his brows are furrowed and he is looking down at a piece of paper on the table. He is biting on his lip as he does when he is stressed out and is tapping a pen on the table. Riley is sitting across from him with his hands under his chin, propping up his head.

I can see Cooper getting more and more annoyed by the second; the look on his face becomes more and more contorted until he reaches over, grabs his coffee, picks it up, and chucks it across the cafe. It flies through the air and slams against the wall opposite them, steaming hot coffee exploding all over the place.

This has to be a dream, I think. I can hear my own voice echoing around me.

I open my mouth and try to yell out to Cooper, but no sound comes out. I have nothing more than an inner monologue. I try to wave my arms around to get his attention, but it's as if he can't see me. He even looks up directly at me, but doesn't acknowledge my existence.

Suddenly, I hear an engine revving heavily behind me and turn to look, only to be blinded by bright LED headlights. I raise an arm to cover my eyes, but it doesn't help very much; I can't even make out the type of vehicle in front of me. It starts revving harder and louder and I can hear the tires squealing as they slip on the asphalt below. All of a sudden, the lights begin getting closer and closer to me. My legs loosen up and I'm able to dive out of the way just in time for the vehicle to make contact with the glass on the front of the coffee house and the sound of glass shattering pierces the air. I throw my arms up to shield my face from the glass flying,and as I look up to check on Cooper and Riley, I can see them backed into a corner of the dining room. The driver's side door of the vehicle opens and a tall man, dressed in all black with a hood over his head, exits with a gun in his left hand. He raises it and points it at Cooper, who immediately throws his hands up.

Why doesn't Cooper have his *gun?* I wonder.

I sit and helplessly watch from the window like I did when Tom had Cooper's parents tied up. I feel like any move at this moment could spook the man and he'd fire a shot at one of us. That won't help anything right now, so all I can do is watch. The man raises the gun in the air, then looks back at me and fires nine shots into the ceiling. Then again. And again. How many bullets are in that magazine? Nightmare logic.

This continues over and over again; the man never points the gun at Cooper again. The sound of the shots start fading and sounding more like a knock on a door than gunshots.

***

My eyes pop open and suddenly I'm wide awake and there is a frantic knocking on our hotel door. I try to adjust to my surroundings and drag myself out of bed. The knocking continues non-stop until I reach the door.

"Hold on," I say sleepily and slightly annoyed.

I open the door to find a disheveled looking brunette girl standing in the hallway. She looks familiar, but I can't place her. You can tell she's gorgeous, but right now, she has dark circles around her eyes from her makeup running and I can tell she's been crying hard. Her cheeks are bright red and she keeps looking from left to right down the hallway as if someone had just been chasing her.

"Can I come in?" she asks, panicked, "please?"

"Don't let him find me," she says even more panicked. I can hear the shaking in her voice and I look down to see her hands trembling with fear.

"Who?" I ask apathetically.

"The killer," she says as she starts sobbing again.

I stand out of the way and wave her into my room. I don't know who I just let in, but I have a feeling that it wasn't the smartest move I've ever made. She walks into the room and sits on the end of the bed with the palms of her hands to her face as she tries to stifle her cries.

"Who are you?" I ask as I close and lock the door.

"My name is Alicia," she says.

CHAPTER FORTY-FIVE

COOPER COBB

Riley and I are sitting in the back corner booth of the Milan Coffee Station. We are discussing what our next course of action should be to take down the so-called Knock Knock Killer. I almost can't bring myself to call him—or them—that. They're not him. They don't follow his process, and as far as I'm concerned, this person, or persons, are just cheap knockoffs of a mostly successful serial killer.

Delilah left us. She said she didn't feel well and wanted to go back to the hotel we booked on the way here. I don't feel right making plans without my partner in crime, but this needs to be done. We need to find a way to defeat this evil.

I look around the café and observe the people around us. They all seem to be leading totally normal lives. There's a group of friends laughing and telling jokes across from us, there is a couple who look like they're on a first date, and there's a couple of people sitting in a corner sipping on shots of espresso while they read. It all feels peaceful, and it's a gentle reminder that, outwardly, we can all seem like everything is okay, while inside, it's all falling apart.

"I'm going to taunt him with a live episode," I say, "like we did last time."

"That's so boring," Riley says, "you can't have the same climax. It needs to be bigger. Better."

I stare at him with annoyance. He means well, but I don't think he sees the seriousness in the situation we find ourselves in.

"Are you okay?" I ask.

"What do you mean?" he asks.

"I mean, your girlfriend is missing—kidnapped by the killer and you haven't mentioned her since we left her house."

He looks down at the table, refusing to make eye contact with me. I can see the hurt in his eyes and the fear on his face. His first real relationship and this happens; it can't be easy on him.

"Just trying not to think about it," he says, but I can see he hasn't stopped thinking of her. "Besides, how the hell am I supposed to help her? I don't have a clue where she is. I don't even know where to start."

"That's why I'm saying we need to taunt him. If we taunt him, he will use her as bait. If he's anything like Tom, I can almost predict his next move."

As soon as the words leave my lips, I look up and see two bright LEDs coming quickly toward the building. I don't even have time to warn anyone before a large vehicle comes crashing through the front window of the small town café. It's like an explosion; shards of glass fly through the air as the black battering ram destroys everything in its path, sending chairs and tables flying across the room. I grab Riley and pull him and myself into a corner while we throw our arms up over our faces to avoid being sliced open by the shards of the window.

The truck is only stopped by the back wall of the café; the smell of gasoline and other fluids fill the air and sting my nose. I put my arm up over my nose as I try to catch my breath thand see through the smoke and debris littering the once peaceful atmosphere that the Milan Coffee Station brought. I look around and several people are lying on the ground. Many are screaming and crying out in pain and fear. One man is lying face down on the floor, bleeding heavily from his head.

"Riley, are you okay?" I ask.

"I'm fine," he says.

"Okay, I'll be right back." I run over to the bleeding man when the driver's side door opens to the vehicle. A tall man in a black robe and hood covering his face emerges from the dust. Looking right at me, he raises his arm and points a nine-millimeter pistol toward me. He doesn't say a word. Just looks at me and threatens through his actions to shoot me dead right here and now.

I back up and grab the holster hanging off of my hip and quickly draw my gun and point it back at him. Without thinking, I pull the trigger, but with the adrenaline coursing through my veins causing my hand to shake, I miss my mark by two inches. It gives him the opportunity to pull the trigger on his firearm. From behind me, I hear a scream and look over to see Riley has been shot in the arm.

I instantly holster my gun, not thinking of the implications of such an action and tend to Riley. Pressing hard on the wound. I grab his arm and look at where the bullet went in. It went straight through and lodged itself into the wall behind him. Tears are streaming down his face as I apply pressure to it.

I look behind me and the man has disappeared. There is no trace of him anywhere. It seems he disappeared into thin air. I turn back to Riley and continue to hold pressure to his bullet hole. In the distance, I can already hear sirens coming toward us, and it doesn't take long to see blinding flashing red lights outside.

Police, EMS, and fire personnel quickly swarm the building to assess the damage. I wave one of them over to us to signal that we have an injury over here and they swiftly come to Riley's side. I let go of his arm and back away to ensure they have room to do their job.

The dust has mostly settled with just a little bit continuing to float in the air, but the vehicle inside the building is smoking, so the fire department urges everyone to vacate the premises. I happily oblige and as I step through what was once the front window to the café, almost tripping over the rubble, I'm met with a familiar face.

"Mr. Cobb," Detective Prescott says.

"Detective?" I yell with surprise in my voice.

I reach my hand out to shake his, and he barely acknowledges my nicety.

"Mr. Cobb, I was just about to call you when we got the call for this," he says as he gestures to the building. The look on his face is solemn as if he feels bad for me.

"What's going on?" I ask.

"You need to come with me," he says.

"But Riley—"

"Riley will be fine. Come with me," he says, more forcefully this time.

CHAPTER FORTY-SIX

DELILAH CARNEY

"Like, *Alicia*, Alicia?" I ask.

Alicia gives me a puzzled look, almost as if she doesn't know what or whom I am referring to. I stare at her blankly. I have so many questions to ask, yet nothing will come out of my mouth. I inspect her up and down like I'm checking her out. I look up and down several times. She is dirty, sweaty, her makeup is running, and her cheeks are red. I spot blood on her hands. I can't imagine what she's gone through, yet I have a feeling I know everything. I sit down on the bed next to her.

"You're…" I start, "you're Riley's girlfriend, Alicia?" I ask, but I know the answer and it comes out more as a confirmation.

She nods. "Yes," she says, "where is he?"

"Him and Cooper are at the Coffee Station working out a plan," I say.

We sit in silence for a moment, and I inspect her further. There is a small twitch at the corner of her eye when I say Cooper's name and it makes me suspicious of her. I try to scoot over without alerting her, to keep the distance between us.

"Oh," she says.

"So, what happened to you?" I ask.

"I really don't know," she says, "one moment I was sitting in my room and the next, I was waking up on a dusty, dirty concrete floor. My phone was sitting next to me, which I found really strange. What kind of kidnapper leaves their victim with a phone? I could've called anyone, but I didn't really know where I was, so I called Riley when I came to."

"...And here we are," I say, "once again, trying to take down a mass murderer."

I say it in a lighthearted way, trying to be funny, but Alicia doesn't see the humor in it; in fact, she looks annoyed that she's even sitting here with me right now. I need to find a way to get away from her—she's making me more and more uncomfortable by the minute and I'm not sure why.

"Give me a moment," I say and stand up from the bed, "I need to run to the bathroom and change real quick. I don't think pajamas are appropriate with company."

Alicia gives me a half smile and I turn quickly and walk away toward the bathroom, then close and lock the door. I look at myself in the mirror for a moment. I, too, have seen better days. I feel like this little being inside me is draining every bit of energy out of my body and my visage gives it away, too.

I assess the clothes I have sitting on the counter and begin to undress. I look down at my stomach once again—I swear I can see a bump. I proceed to throw my new clothes on. I'm not sure why I'm throwing on such nice clothes, but I think the escape to the bathroom is nothing more than nervous energy. Alicia's abrupt arrival has put me on edge, as if I wasn't already. I don't even know this girl, and I already don't like her for Riley, but I'm not his mom; I don't get an opinion.

I finish getting dressed and look at myself in the mirror again. I look a little more put together now; at least it's better than the pajama pants and oversized t-shirt I was wearing. Now I'm wearing Cooper's old Ice Nine Kills shirt that is too small for him and white jeans. I reach for the door handle and pause for a moment. I close my eyes and take a deep breath. In, then out. I turn the handle and exit the bathroom.

As I walk out, I feel a massive thud on the side of my skull and a sharp pain shoots through my entire head. I fall to the ground in pain, wailing and crying out in agony.

What the fuck just hit me?

I look up and try to adjust my eyes by blinking multiple times, but blurriness has taken over. I see a figure step over me holding a large object, but I can't make out who it is or what it is that they're holding, though I can guess *who* it is.

"Alicia, what the f—" I start to say as she hits me again.

The world begins to spin and I can see blackness coming into my field of vision from the edges, slowly making its way inward. I'm going to go unconscious and there is nothing I can do to stop it.

"This is for Tatum," she says, before hitting me over the head one last time and my entire world spins, then grinds to a halt. The slowly fading blackness takes over and for only another moment I can hear the tone of the room around me and the heavy breathing over my limp, almost lifeless body. I beg in my head for God to take me now, but before I can finish my pleading, everything grinds to a halt.

CHAPTER FORTY-SEVEN

COOPER COBB

Detective Prescott drives in silence down Route 113 toward Berlinville. He won't tell me where we are going and I decide not to ask. I already have a bad feeling in the pit of my stomach. There is only one reason why he would make me come with him and we would be taking this road; mentally, I'm already preparing for the worst. He made me sit in the backseat, so I stare out the window and zone into the cornfields whizzing past us. I feel like a prisoner back here, and, point in fact, the last time I was in the back of one of these vehicles behind the grate was when Delilah and I had been arrested on suspicion of being involved in Tom and Tatum's killings.

I want to call Delilah or Riley and check in, but I can't right now—I feel completely disconnected from the two of them, which hasn't happened in months, at least with her. I look out the driver's side rear window and the scenery isn't much different than what I was looking at on the passenger seat. Corn field after corn field, a cemetery: *the* cemetery. A chill runs down my spine remembering what happened there.

After what feels like forever, we pull into a driveway and I have to physically shake my head to drag myself out of my stupor. I look around and all I can see are blinding red and blue lights flashing in the driveway, but it doesn't take me too long to realize, even though I already knew where we ended up. We are at my parents and as Detective Prescott gets out, comes around, and lets me out of the backseat, my worst fears have come alive. I look around and observe the chaos around the house. An ambulance and a few police cars, but then I spot it, the coroner's van. My heart jumps into my throat and my stomach turns. I turn my head to the right and suddenly the contents of my stomach are on the ground. I gag and cough, then lift my head back up and wipe my mouth on my sleeve.

"Detective, is it my mom or my dad?" I ask, as if I think he's really going to tell me.

"I think it's best you just go inside, Cooper, but I'm warning you: it's not pretty," he says.

I take a deep breath and march up to the front door, pausing for a moment before entering. The door frame is still damaged from Tom kicking it in and there is a small chunk of wood missing from the impact. I run my fingers over it for a moment, though I'm not sure why; probably to delay the inevitable. I put on a brave face and step through the threshold and I see my mom sitting on the couch crying her eyes out, and at that moment, I know. I know exactly what happened. She's sitting with a towel on her head and wearing her bathrobe as though she had just stepped out of the shower. I walk into the room and she spots me almost instantly.

"Oh, Cooper," she says, putting a hand over her mouth.

I look down on the floor and my dad's body is lying there lifeless with a pool of blood surrounding him, already soaking into the carpet beneath him. His eyes are still open and crime scene investigators are marking the scene and taking photos of the horror in front of them. Many of them move swiftly without speaking. The atmosphere is somber, of course, ghostly almost. It doesn't feel real, but at the same time, I don't feel anything. Am I just so desensitized to death that even my own father's demise doesn't affect me?

I just stare at his body, the blood has drained from his face already and he is pale as a ghost. I look up at my mom who is simply beside herself. I make my way around, carefully avoiding the equipment and his body and sit down next to my mom who immediately throws her arms around me, whispering in my ear.

"Make it stop," she says.

"I don't know how this time." I reply.

She lets go of me and backs off, simply staring me in the eyes as if I will magically come up with an answer or a plan of some sort. I just stare back at her and watch as she furrows her brows and her expression changes from that of a grieving wife to a pissed off spouse.

"You did this," she says, "*you* fix it."

She reaches out to smack me, but before her hand can make contact with my cheek, I reach out and grab her arm and stand up, still holding on to her. I ball my hand up into a fist and pull back, ready to swing at her. I've never thought about punching my own mother, but right now, with that accusation and my father being deceased, what more could I lose?

I think about the police being nearby, and I think about the consequences if I do assault her, then lower my fist. I could lose everything, and that includes Delilah, and I can't let that happen. I stare at my mother for another brief moment, considering my next words wisely, though I'm not entirely sure what to say to her. There are so many things I *want* to say, but don't know if she is worth wasting my breath on.

"Fuck you, bitch," I say, finally finding the words that are worth saying, "*you* did this. *You* let Tom go, *you* caused all of this. Take some fucking responsibility for once in your pitiful, pathetic life."

I turn on my heels and walk out of the house, but not before I notice something on the inside of the door that has been left slightly ajar from everyone walking in and out. I grab the door and pull it half-shut. What I see on the door takes me back to the night we found Delilah's family dead. I look at it for a moment and I shake my head. This person is just copying Tom at this point and I have to hold back a chuckle as I read the words written in blood on the door: *Knock Knock Cooper*.

I step out onto the front porch, pull out my phone, and immediately dial Delilah, but I get her voicemail. I try to call Riley, but get the same result. I'm more worried about her than him; her, I left alone, but he was with paramedics and police. He should be fine. I walk back up to Detective Prescott.

"Cooper, I'm sorry, bud," he says.

"I also wanted to say I'm sorry. About Detective Carpenter," I say, finally showing my sorrow and remorse for his untimely death.

"Thanks," he says, as a tear rolls down his cheek.

"Can you find out if Riley is still at the Coffee Station? I need to get back to him."

"Sure thing," he says as he steps away to radio someone.

I step out into the middle of the yard, still feeling mostly emotionless. I sit down in the grass and rub the soft blades on the palms of my hands for a moment and look up to the pitch black nothingness of space. It's a clear night, not a single cloud in sight. I inspect the stars above. It's been a long time since I just took a moment to reflect and be at peace with nature. The moon is just bright enough to shine down on the front yard like a spotlight is beaming down onto me. I close my eyes and drift into my own thoughts. I can't help but wonder what life would be like if none of this were happening. I believe everything happens for a reason; it's an old cliche, but I wholeheartedly believe in it. Would I be with Delilah? Would my life have any adventure? That's what all of this is—an adventure, just in the way you hope your life is adventurous.

Just as I find myself almost fully at peace, my phone begins to vibrate in my pocket and I am pulled back to reality. I reach into my pocket and pull it out. It's a text from the unknown person, something I haven't received in quite a while now. I open up the text and it's a dark photo; it's almost impossible to make out what it's of. Then I spot it, dead center. It's Delilah tied to a chair. Her head is tilted down and she looks like she's passed out. I can see some blood droplets on the leg of her pants. Though she's hurt, she's clearly still alive.

My heart is racing and I place a hand over my chest as if it's about to beat through my ribcage and land on the ground in front of me. I stand up, but my world is spinning and my breathing gets faster and heavier. I'm alone. I don't know what to do. I can't alert the police. They have her. They're going to kill her, I'm sure of it. I need to get back to Riley and together we need to find her, but how? Then another text comes through. I look down at my phone again.

You'll find her where you fucked her! How fast are you, Cobb? Can you find her before we kill her?

If they think they're Tom, then they will wait. This is bait. They're using her as bait to get to me. I know they'll wait to kill her in front of me. I have time. Where is Riley? Shakily, I try to call him again, but it goes to voicemail.

"Fuck!" I yell. A few of the police officers and paramedics whip their heads around and look at me.

I spot Prescott and run up to him.

"Did you find Riley?" I ask.

"He's at the hospital, I'll take you to him," he says.

I look around and see the coroner wheeling my dad out on a gurney and loading him up into the back of the van. My mom is standing on the top step crying again as they do it. For a moment, I feel bad for her and I consider running up to her and giving her a big hug. I can't. *She* did this. *She* started this and *I* will end it. Before Prescott can even wave me over, I'm running to the car, opening the door to the backseat. Just before I close the door, I yell at him.

"Let's go," I say, "Now."

CHAPTER FORTY-EIGHT

DELILAH CARNEY

Darkness. Pure darkness. The sound of dripping in the corner of the room. I try to open my eyes, but they're tired. I'm tired. I keep nodding in and out of consciousness. I can't stay awake long enough to evaluate the situation I've found myself in.

Where am I?

I force my eyes open and attempt to look around, but it's all dark. I can't see a damn thing, and on top of that, I have a pounding migraine. Maybe it's for the best that it's dark. I try to move my arms, but they won't budge and I can feel something giving me what feels like rug burn on my wrists. I maneuver my fingers on one hand to try to feel what it is. It feels like a rope. I try to move my legs, but same thing, except I don't feel the intense burning on my skin. It's become clear that my ankles are tied to the chair I'm sitting in, too.

I've seen enough horror movies to know that I am completely fucked right now. The only thing I can do is wait for someone to come in that will inevitably torture me and taunt me until I can't take anymore and they decide to kill me.

Drip.

Drip.

Drip.

That pipe dripping is driving me nuts, but there is nothing I can do but try to keep it out of my mind and figure out a plan. These ropes are tied so damn tight that I can't maneuver my hands enough to try to get free.

Wait.

I assess the chair I'm sitting in. It's made of wood and I've seen this before. If I tip over, it could break; of course, I could hit my head on the floor and knock myself out again—but it's worth the risk.

The baby.

No, I can't think about that right now. I can't save our baby if I don't try to save myself. I'm a sitting duck right now, just waiting for my own demise. I try to figure out the room I'm in, but I can't see a single thing right now. If I do get free, I need a plan. I need to figure out a way out of here, but it seems there aren't even any windows here, or they're blocked so no light comes through. Maybe if I get free I can figure it out from there. I start to rock the chair side to side. With each rock I can feel the legs going further and further. One more.

I fall to the ground with a thud, but the chair doesn't break.

"Shit!" I yell, but just as I do, I hear a door creak open nearby. I stay still and silent as if the person who put me here won't find me just because I'm horizontal and not vertical as they left me.

The inside of my mouth tastes like metal, like I've been sucking on pennies; I think my mouth is bleeding. I listen intently and can hear stairs creaking as someone is coming down them slowly, then a light splash when they hit the bottom. The leaking pipe is leaving a puddle on the hard concrete ground. I can hear the squelching of the water with each step they take as it gets louder and louder, closer and closer to me. I snap my eyes shut and close them tightly as I anticipate my final moments.

Instead, the footsteps come right in front of me and I can feel a pair of hands grabbing on to me, then lifting the chair back upright. I can feel their hot breath right in front of me as they come face to face with me; I just wish I could fucking see *something*. They're doing something; I can hear them shuffling. I just wish they would talk to me, but then I can hear Cooper's voice echoing in my head.

"Poke the bear, Delilah," I hear him say to me as if he is standing here with me, so I say the first thing I can think of.

"You must think you're really big and bad, don't you?" I say. Not the most intimidating line I could come up with, but the best I have under the stress.

They laugh—it's a deep guttural laugh, but with a higher pitch to it.

"Welcome," she starts, "to the *Knock Knock Podcast* with Delilah Carney." She says it with a condescending tone to her voice.

"You forgot Cooper Cobb," I say, correcting her.

"No, no, Delilah. You're the main attraction right now, not him."

She's still messing around with something. I can hear some light thunking as if she's setting something up, then a beep and a red light.

"Real original. You're going to record my murder?" I say, trying to sound tough, but freaking out inside. "That's real Jigsaw-killer of you."

She turns around and faces me again. Even though I can't see anything, I can tell by the sound of her voice that she's looking at me.

"No, you see, when you and Cooper killed Tom, Cooper livestreamed the whole thing. Well, now, the tables are turned. We are live streaming *your* deaths."

"Well, I hate to break it to you, but Cooper isn't here," I say, "it's just me."

"In due time, he will arrive thinking he's coming to save the day again, but I'm here to tell you it's different this time. It's different because we are ready for him."

I hear the door open again, and this time, I can hear where it is coming from. I think I'm in a basement somewhere. I can't say where, but that has narrowed it down just a little bit. I have something to go off of. The door slams shut and I can hear the walls shake above me. Footsteps begin on the stairs, but this time they're heavier. I'd say it's a man this time. As he makes his way down, she gets closer to my face and I can feel her breath on me again. I wish I could remember what happened back at the hotel. I remember answering the door and then…

Alicia, I think, *shit.*

"Know this, Delilah. He won't show up until *we* want him to because we want to have some fun with you first. You deserve it. You deserve it, because you killed her."

"Now, Alicia, she deserves to know everything. Be a better hostess to our guest."

I know that voice. Why do I know that voice?

CHAPTER FORTY-NINE

COOPER COBB

I want to grab Detective Prescott's leg and slam it down onto the accelerator as hard as I can. How can someone who is a cop drive so slow? There's only a couple of issues with that plan; one, I'd probably be arrested, and two, this stupid grate between us. I don't know why I opted to sit in the back seat when I had the opportunity to be up front. I'm not under arrest.

We pull up to the hospital and I attempt to pull on the door handle as hard as I can, as if it will open from the inside—I know it won't, but I continue to pull anyway. I can feel the little piece of plastic wanting to give way and snap in half. Prescott gets out of the car and saunters around to my side and before he can barely pull the door open, I push it, knocking him off-balance.

"Sorry," I say as I run into the hospital, barely looking back at him.

"Cobb," he yells at me, and it stops me in my tracks, "if you know something, tell me now. I don't want you getting involved."

The truth is, this time around, I don't know anything. I know the bastard hurt my best friend in a failed attempt to kill us both, and I know that he, or she, or they killed my dad, but that's it. I don't know what I'm going to do or how I'm going to do it. I just know I need to get to Riley, then to Delilah before it's too late, before things get even worse. I shake my head at Prescott and he shuts the back door to his car and simply nods at me.

Just before I enter the front door, my phone begins to ring and I pull it out of my pocket cautiously. I look at the screen and it's a video call from Delilah—there's no way that's possible. I answer the call and the loading circle spins and spins on the screen. I begin to tap my foot as my patience wears thin with the crappy cell signal, then an image pops up on screen and my mouth drops immediately and tears begin to roll down my cheeks. My mom's voice echoes in my head as I hear her say, "*You* did this."

In front of me is Delilah tied to the same chair I saw in the photo with a bright light shining down on her. She has her head slumped forward and I can see blood dripping from her mouth. From out of the frame, a figure steps in to where I can see them, and they're holding something. It looks like a thin piece of wood. The person raises it up, points it at the camera, then raises it over Delilah's head, swinging it down. With a loud smack, it hits her in the back of the neck and her head slumps down slightly. She's barely conscious now.

I wince as the smack comes through the phone, then a second person steps into the frame and puts a hand up, signaling the other person to stop what they're doing for a moment, then both turn to look at the camera, though I can't see their faces. They are covered by black hoods. I wipe the tears out of my eyes then look away for a moment, looking toward the door to the hospital. Do I go inside and get Riley, or do I leave him and go to her?

I don't even know where she is.

The thought crosses my mind and I realize that now, more than ever, I need Riley's help. I look back at the screen awaiting some sort of grand finale, but it doesn't come. They continue to stare into the screen, taunting me, waiting for me to figure out their strange little riddle.

You'll find her, *where you fucked* her, I think, but it doesn't make any sense. Our old house here in Milan? Is that where they are with Delilah? It can't be. There's a new family living there. How could they even pull off something like that? But that *is* the place where we did it for the first time, just before moving out.

I'm staring at her; she looks tired, she looks completely destroyed, but what can I do? Tears begin to roll down my face again and I turn the phone away so they can't see that I am crying. Now isn't the time to show a shred of weakness. I make sure my face is clear, then turn the phone back toward me, putting on a brave face; I try to look and sound as arrogant as I can.

"Pansy bitches," I say to the screen, "looks like you did take over for Tom. He was just as big of a pussy as the two of you. Don't have the balls to come for me? You always have to go for those that I love the most?"

The person on the left of the screen begins to speak. "Don't you remember what happened when Tom attacked your parents? You came to their rescue. It's only a matter of time before you try to do the same for *her*, but there is a difference between us and Tom. We are going to kill you and we are going to make her watch as you bleed out on the floor," the man says as he points a knife at Delilah.

"Cooper," Delilah's weak voice says, "leave me, don't come here."

The other person on the right side of the screen balls their hand up into a fist and punches Delilah in the face, swinging her head to the side as blood flies from her mouth. Delilah sputters and gags, then spits blood at them.

"So, what's this all about this time?" I ask, "is this just old-fashioned copycat serial murders or what?"

"Oh, a motive? You want a motive?" a female's voice asks. "Revenge, simply put, of course."

"Revenge for what? Killing that piece of shit brother of mine? What was he to you?" I say, demanding an answer.

"You will have your answer in due time," the man says, "but you have to find us first."

The female walks up to the phone and ends the video call as I'm standing outside of this hospital by myself. Where do I start? I need to go inside and get Riley and try to get him out of here. I need his help.

CHAPTER FIFTY

RILEY STEVENS

The best way I can describe being shot is like someone throwing a small pebble at my body. It didn't feel like anything. I felt the impact, but felt no pain at first. The adrenaline coursing through my veins blocked my brain from feeling anything. I remember screaming, but I think it was the fear that shot through me when the gunshot rang through the air. It felt like someone took their palm and pushed me, knocking me over. That's it. I've heard the nurses here mentioning shock, which makes sense to me now. By the time Cooper took off and the paramedics came to my side, I could feel it. They said it was a through and through wound in the arm and that I should be fine, but the pain that followed the shock was immense—it still is. They have me on some painkillers, but nothing crazy, which surprises me. They basically gave me a strong Motrin, which isn't what I'd expect someone getting prescribed after being shot.

I look around the stale room; bright lights hang above me and a heart monitor beeps in the corner. I glance at it: eighty beats per minute. I have a needle stuck in the top of my hand with a saline solution running into my veins to keep me hydrated. Every now and then, an emergency department nurse pokes her head in around the curtain, asks how I'm doing, then swiftly leaves again. Oddly enough, though I'm recovering from a bullet wound, this is the most relaxed I've felt in weeks. It's the safest I've felt, but I can't stop thinking about Alicia and how scared she must be. I need to get out of here and find her, but I can't do it alone. I need Cooper and Delilah.

As if he could read my thoughts, suddenly Cooper appears from behind the curtains, sweaty and out of breath with a nurse following closely behind him.

"I'm sorry Mr. Stevens, I tried to stop him, I told him you couldn't have visitors."

Cooper places his hands on his knees trying to catch his breath, panting heavily.

"It's okay, he can stay," I say.

The nurse, looking extremely annoyed, turns on her heels and leaves, pulling the curtain behind her and then I hear her say "Cancel security." I look at Cooper, then immediately burst into laughter. The way he barreled in here with the nurse right behind him looking like she was about to launch herself and tackle him is hysterical to me, but he looks back up at me with a serious look and my laughter stops almost as quick as it started.

"What is it?" I ask as the smile slowly fades from my face.

"You need to get out of here. We need to go," he says.

"Dude," I say, annoyed, pointing at the bullet hole and the IV sticking out of my arm.

"They have Delilah," he says, "they're torturing her. They're playing some sick game with me. With us."

He continues to stare at me with severity on his face. I know he wouldn't joke about this, but part of me wants to believe that it is a joke. I study him for a moment, then consider my options. If I get out of here, I want to go look for Alicia, but at the same time, I've known Delilah longer. Truth be told, I'm torn on what to do.

"Do you know who they are?" I ask.

He shakes his head, then pulls out his phone and makes his way over to the bed, handing the phone over to me. He received a text earlier this evening from the killer, or killers, or whoever is behind this. I read it and it's like a lightbulb is going off in my brain. I have an idea and I think I know who it is now, or at least where they have Delilah.

"We have to go," I say as I reach over to my arm and start ripping the IV tube out of my body and start taking off the heart monitors, ripping chest hair with each pull and wincing from the hair being pulled out of my follicles. Cooper reaches over and pulls the last one out which makes me audibly yelp in pain. A smile curves at the edges of his mouth—it's the first smile I've seen on his face in weeks. I start to run out of the room, but I realize I'm still wearing a hospital gown and grippy socks, so I turn around and grab my clothes out of the plastic drawstring bag the hospital gave me.

"Give me two minutes," I say.

"Dude, are you feeling okay? I need your help but if you're not feeling right, I don't want you to exert," Cooper says.

"I'm well enough, and you need me," I say, then look back at him again, "and I think I might know where they are."

"Wait how do you—" Cooper begins to say, but I run into the bathroom and close the door mid-sentence.

I throw on my clothes, which proves to be a more daunting task than I imagined. I have weakened muscles in my arm from the bullet wound paired with adrenaline coursing through my veins. We are about to face off against another couple of killers, but this time, I'm in the thick of it, and I have more to lose this time around. I finish up and assess my appearance in the mirror, ensuring that I think I look well enough to tackle this because it's going to be a fight.

I swing the door open and practically run back into the room and right past Cooper before stopping and waving him over. I peek around the curtain to see if I can make a clean getaway, but there are nurses everywhere. There's no way I'm going to be able to escape without being noticed, so I do the only thing I can think of: I pull the curtain back quickly and bolt through the emergency department with Cooper directly on my heels. I can hear the nurse that has been tending to me all night yelling behind us, but I don't stop. We need to keep going.

We finally reach the front door to the hospital and we keep running. I might be in worse shape than I thought I was because I am getting winded much quicker than I normally would. Once we think we are in the clear and completely off the hospital's property, we stop for a moment to catch our breath.

"Dude," Cooper says, "what the *hell* was that?"

"They weren't going to release me so we had to make a clean break."

"Okay, so how do you know where to find them?" he asks.

"I don't," I say, "but think about it. Think about the text you got. 'You'll find *her* where you fucked *her.*'"

I'm looking at Cooper as if I'm expecting him to understand what I'm saying, but the look on his face tells me he's still confused. I put emphasis on the words when I said it, but he's not understanding. The one who is supposed to be good at working these riddles out can't seem to comprehend that we were already at where we needed to be, just much sooner.

"Dude," I say, slapping Cooper on the shoulder, "Tatum's house—err, Alicia's house, now."

CHAPTER FIFTY-ONE

DELILAH CARNEY

The light shining in my eyes is blinding me. They just ended the call with Cooper. I wish I could see them. I wish I could lay eyes on those who are about to end my life, but they don't want me to know who they are. It's weird that she would continue to hide her face. Does she think I don't remember who she is? Are they afraid they can't finish the job and I'll report them and get their asses thrown in jail?

"Taunt them, poke the bear," I can hear Cooper saying in my head.

Alicia walks up to me, gently places a couple of fingers under my chin, and lifts my head up. I'm too weak to lift it on my own. I maneuver my eyes to her face, studying what I can see. If I make it out of this, I want to be able to describe my attacker. The unfortunate thing is that all I can see is from under her eyes to her chin and all I have is a first name. She begins to speak to me.

"Beautiful, lovely Delilah," she says, "it's a shame we have to kill you."

I rear back and blow a blood-filled loogie at her face as she's closing her mouth and it lands on her tongue. She steps back in surprise and pulls out her gun. I can feel my eyes wanting to widen out of sheer surprise, but I keep it together. I can't let her know that she's getting to me. I can't let her think I fear her.

"Fuck you, bitch," I say as my head falls back down and I'm staring at my feet.

She presses the gun to my head and I wince as the pressure of the cold metal touches my scalp. I shut my eyes as tight as I can. If this is it, I don't want to know when it's happening.

"Well, c'mon, what are you waiting for? Shoot me," I say, continuing to piss her off. I can see through her body language that she is getting antsy. The bright light is still shining down on me and through squinted eyes, I can see the entirety of their bodies.

Suddenly, a loud bang fills my ear canals, followed by a resounding, high-pitched ringing. She pulled the trigger, but I'm still here. I check my body the best I can, then pain in my right shoulder begins to sear through my entire arm and into my back. I look over and can see blood running from the fresh wound. I close my eyes tightly to fight the pain, but there is no longer a way for me to hide that I am hurting. Tears begin to roll down my face. I bite onto my bottom lip to try to stop the crying, but she sees and I can hear her laughing.

"Alicia!" I hear the man yell, "Not yet!"

"Come on dad, can't we just kill this stupid skank?"

I look up at her with disdain, but I can't help but catch that one little word in her voice. *Dad.* I think I'm having a revelation now. I think I've figured it out. Are they…? They can't be. I shake the thought out of my mind. Tatum lived on her own…I think. I find some bravery deep within the pits of my soul and begin to laugh maniacally.

"What's so funny?" Alicia says.

"It's funny you call me that. I've been with one man and one man only—Cooper. But Tatum, man, she would spread her legs for anyone, wouldn't she?"

WHACK!

I feel a pounding and a stinging on the back of my head. My sight begins to blur, the room begins to spin, then, nothing. Darkness. Then the light pierces my field of vision again as I nod in and out of consciousness.

"Is that the best you've got?" I ask, sleepily.

CHAPTER FIFTY-TWO

COOPER COBB

As we turn onto the street, the final stretch, my heart races. It could be the anxiety, or it could just be that I haven't run like this in ages. My head begins to spin and now I know this is the beginning of a panic attack. I come to a dead stop quickly in the middle of the road and Riley, who isn't too far behind me, slams into my back.

"Dude, what the hell? Let's go!" he shouts at me.

"Give…me…a…minute," I say to him between breaths.

I have my hands resting on my knees as I pant and try to catch my breath. I look up and I can see a familiar scene in the distance. The single street light illuminates the atmosphere just enough that I can faintly make out the facade of Tatum's old house. This doesn't help with the panic, rather, it intensifies it. I stare into the distance and simply ponder. If Riley is wrong about this, if he is even a hair wrong, Delilah could be dead before we find her. This is our only answer at this time. We have to hope and pray against all odds that we are right.

I stand up straight and crack my neck and my knuckles. My breathing is returning to normal now. I take one last deep, long breath, then exhale slowly and with purpose. I furrow my brows. It's game time. This has to be it. We *have* to find her.

"You ready, Coop?" Riley asks while putting a hand on my shoulder.

"Yeah," I say as I pull my handgun from its holster and cock it, putting a bullet in the chamber, ready for anything. "Let's do this."

We start running for the house again and when we finally reach the yard, we both stop dead in our tracks. The entire home is dark—eerily dark, but there is one exception. I can see a faint light emitting from one of the egress windows that look into the basement. Slowly, quietly, I make my way to the window, attempting not to give away my presence. As I peek in the window, I see her. She is tied to a chair and looks like she's been beaten up pretty bad. Even in this state, she's beautiful as ever. I look to my left and Riley is already walking up the front steps in an attempt to check the front door.

He grabs the handle, but it's locked. We need to find another way in. We sneak away from the basement window and make our way around the back of the house where we find a trellis. There are vines growing up it, but I think I can see a way we might be able to get a hold of it, climb up, and try to sneak into a bedroom window. I holster my gun and start climbing.

"What are you doing?" Riley says with a hushed tone.

"It's the only way we are going to get in," I say, "come on."

To his dismay, he begins to climb. I can hear him struggling beneath me, but I'm having an easy time with it. I get up to the roof and lay on my stomach, reaching down to grab his hand and help him up. We get to our feet and look around. I would recognize that room anywhere, as if the scenery is burned into my brain, but it also won't disorient me when I enter the home. I run over to Tatum's old bedroom window and try it, but it's locked, too.

"What are we going to do now?" Riley asks.

I place my hands on my hips and think for a moment. I'm not entirely sure what to do either. So I decide to make one of the ballsiest moves I've ever made in my life, besides trying to track down and kill serial killers for the second time in less than a year. I reach down, put my hand around my gun, and think for a moment if this is truly what I want to do. If I do this, it's game on, and they will know we are here, or at least know someone is here. I pull the gun out of its holster and aim at the window. From behind me, I can hear Riley muttering "Oh shit, oh shit, oh shit."

BANG!

BANG!

BANG!

CHAPTER FIFTY-THREE

ALICIA

WHACK!

I hit the dumb bitch in the back of the head as hard as I could. How dare she. How *dare* she speak about Tatum that way. Tatum was not a slut. She was a beautiful soul who was taken from this earth far too soon by this trigger happy bitch. Her sins are greater than Tatum's were.

"Is that the best you've got?" she says as her head falls and she goes unconscious again.

I let out a deep triumphant laugh—hopefully that kills her and we can be done with this madness. I'm over it. Dad looks over at me with his face still hiding behind his mask, but I can feel his energy and I can tell he's disappointed that I'm torturing her. He didn't want that; just a few clean kills and get revenge on those that took everything from us. After a long, drawn out silence and us seemingly having a staring contest, he finally speaks up.

"Tatum wouldn't want that, you know," he says.

"Don't act like you know what she would want. You were never around. I was the one that knew her, not you," I say defiantly.

"I knew her well enough," he says, "to know that she wouldn't want you torturing the poor girl."

"Fuck you," I say under my breath.

Out of nowhere, he runs up to me and grabs me by the throat. His temper has always gotten the best of him and this is just another rage fit. I can feel his fingers squeezing tighter every second they remain around my neck, but all I do is smile back at him.

"Do it," I say squeakily, forcing air through my windpipe, "do it."

I challenge him only because I know he won't do it. He won't end me; I'm too valuable to him. He needs me to help him finish this. I think he realizes it too, because he begins to loosen his grip on me, then walks away.

"So, is the plan still to lead them to the cemetery like Tom did?" I ask, acting as if that didn't just happen.

"Yes," he says.

The basement falls silent: so silent you can hear a pin drop on the floor, and for a couple of minutes we don't speak to one another, then he turns and looks at me again. Suddenly, we hear three muffled gunshots through the cinder block walls.

"Plans have changed. It's time," he says, "put your mask back on."

CHAPTER FIFTY-FOUR

DELILAH CARNEY

In an instant, my world went black, then I came back again. My eyesight is blurry and my head is pounding. I can feel cramps in my lower abdomen starting—not too intense, but enough to let me know they're there. I'm looking around the room trying to get my bearings when suddenly I hear something. Even the cinder block walls can't block out the sound.

BANG!

BANG!

BANG!

There's no denying those are gunshots—I think Cooper and Riley have figured out where I am, even though I still have no fucking clue. I blink my eyes rapidly a few times trying to get the blurriness to fade and the world back into focus. I hear the man, who I still don't know the identity of, talking to Alicia. The words are muffled, but I can make them out. It sounds like I'm underwater.

"Plans have changed. It's time, put your mask back on," he says to her.

I lift my head slightly, but it feels like instead of a brain under my skull, it's full of bricks. I'm tired—so tired. I want this to end, but I feel this may just be the end of me. I think about everything Cooper and I could have had. I think about the little one growing in my belly and the life we could have shared. Teaching it to walk, talk, use its manners, overall raising it to be a good person. When you think you're in your final moments, the little things are what matters. I know this now—I wish I'd have realized it sooner.

I can see Alicia scurrying around trying to find her mask, then finding it and slipping it over her head. She runs to her dad's side at the foot of the stairs. Both of them are looking up, standing like statues as the three of us listen intently to the basement ceiling. There are footsteps and they're directly above us. I think about screaming, but that's surely a death sentence. I may still have a chance and I can't risk anything right now.

The door handle to the basement stairs begins to jiggle and my heart begins to race faster by the second. I watch the two of them; just their body language tells me they're panicking. If Cooper and Riley make it down here, they're cornered and it's over. Another bang from upstairs. That's four shots. I know for a fact he only has a ten shot magazine. Six left. Hopefully he grabbed his other magazine.

I can hear something metal clanking down the stairs. It sounds like those videos on TikTok of the guy that rolls random bottles down the stairs and waits to see how long it takes them to break. It hits each stair slowly, but one by one until it rests at Alicia and her dad's feet. They both look down and I look over. My eyes are wide and they turn to look at me. Even behind the masks, I can tell they're panicking.

Suddenly, a slamming sound comes from the top of the stairs, and it must have been both of them at the same time, because the door rips clean off its hinges and flies down the stairs, hitting both Alicia and her dad, knocking them to the ground. Now is my chance.

"Cooper, I'm down here!" I yell at the top of my lungs with every ounce of strength I have left in me.

Alicia and her dad fling the door off them as Cooper and Riley run down the stairs. The killers retreat near me.

"You bitch," Alicia says to me, then pulls out the now famous Buck 119 and plunges it deep into my thigh, turning it counter-clockwise, then clockwise several times.

I scream in agony as the blade rips through flesh and muscle and tears begin to run down my face. She rips it from my flesh and blood begins to soak my white pants, though it's not gushing, so I'm pretty sure she missed the femoral artery.

She runs back to her dad's side as Cooper and Riley are making their way down the stairs. I don't know why Riley came; he's as good as gone—he doesn't have a weapon—but Cooper has his gun drawn pointed right at the two of them. A silence fills the air around us all, then Cooper speaks up.

"Get away from her," he says, "now."

They're at the bottom of the stairs now, and as if he has any power, Riley stands about two steps ahead of Cooper on his right. A smirk forms at the corners of my mouth. I can't believe they found me and I am so happy right now. I know we are far from the end of this, but we are definitely one step closer.

Alicia is holding the knife out ready to pounce the moment one of them lets their guard down, but her hand is shaking. This isn't the ending they planned for at all, and now she's trying to work through some sort of plan—they both are. I can see it the way they are maneuvering around.

"Dee, are you okay?" Cooper asks, not taking his eyes off the two of them.

"I'm fine," I say, weakly.

"Let her go," he starts, "let all of us go and we will let *you* go. I only came here for her. This doesn't have to end the way it did the last time."

He tries negotiating with them, but I don't think that's going to work. I think I've riddled this thing out, but I can't know for sure. I need them to say it out loud. I need their confirmation.

"You're right," the man says, "it's not going to end the same way it did the last time. You're the one who's going to die tonight, Cooper."

Dammit, I know that voice. Why the fuck *do I know that voice?*

"And I'll be the one to do it," Alicia says, finishing her dad's sentence, "I'll be the one that kills you both, and I'm going to do it slowly."

I can see Riley's eyes widen. I think he's figured out it's Alicia and he looks over to me for confirmation. I nod my head solemnly at him and he looks down at the floor. At that moment, he's dropped his guard and Alicia charges at him, not wasting any time, and stabs him in the abdomen. He lets out a yelp as the blade rips through his internal organs and the shock sends him to the ground with her on top of him. She stabs and stabs and stabs, not letting up even for a moment, and blood starts spewing out of Riley's mouth. Cooper is too stunned and opts not to take his attention off the man, but I can see the pain behind his eyes. His best friend is slowly leaving this earth and there's not a thing he can do about it.

Just then, the tiredness hits me again and my eyes begin to slowly close. I try to keep them open. I don't want this to be the last time I see Cooper. I can't have this be the last time I see him, but if it is, I want to remember every detail of him. I glance over at him and his eyes dart toward me filled with concern, then the room turns black again.

***

Within an instant, my eyes pop open again and the fuzziness fills my field of vision once more. I look over to my right and Alicia and her dad are standing at the bottom of the stairs looking up toward the door. I'm confused.

What just happened?

I can hear footsteps on the floor above us. Did I just have one of my weird vision dreams again? Is there a way I can stop Riley from getting stabbed? Is this why I keep having these? Maybe the universe is giving me a chance to redeem myself for teaming up with Tom last time. I thought I was just having weird stress dreams, but it is strange that I've seen a lot happen before it happened. I'm starting to put it together. I'm going to save Riley.

CHAPTER FIFTY-FIVE

COOPER COBB

We reach the stairs that go into the basement. I press my ear against the door, but I can't hear anything. They probably heard our feet making the floorboards squeak. They'll be ready for us and we need to take them off guard. I try the handle, but it's locked. I need to make sure I keep an eye on Riley; he's unarmed. He shouldn't be here, but I know he feels obligated, plus his girlfriend is still missing. We hadn't even discussed her. Our focus has been on saving Delilah. I turn to look at him.

"You ready?" I ask.

"Never," he says with a small, nervous chuckle.

I back up from the door and he does the same, following my every step. I aim my handgun at the handle, hoping this works like it does in the movies. I look back at him one more time and he places a finger in each of his ears. I turn back and make sure to steady my shaking hands, then inhale, exhale, and pull the trigger. The handle on our side of the door flies off and I can hear the handle on the other side falling down the stairs, but the actual bolt itself is still intact inside of the wall; that's not helpful.

"Do you think we could—" I say, but before I can finish, Riley is backing up, readying his shoulder for impact.

"One step ahead of you," he says.

I holster my gun and back up with him and the two of us assume a hunched position, then count down together.

"Three, two, one," we say, then charge at the door shoulders first as hard as we can.

The handle bolt releases and the door flies off its hinges, down the stairs, crashing into two people that were standing at the bottom. I quickly grab for my gun and unholster it again, aiming down the stairs, slowly taking one step at a time. They're quickly getting the door off of them, so we speed up. One of them has already escaped and is running away from the stairs.

"Cooper, I'm down here!" I hear Delilah yell.

I hear another female voice yelling back at her. "You bitch," she says, then I can hear an agonizing scream. Almost to the bottom of the stairs now, the girl comes back to the other person's side. Now at the bottom of the stairs, gun still drawn, the two of them begin to back away from me. It's silent; none of us say a word for a moment, but I'm ready to break that silence.

"Get away from her, now," I say. "Dee, are you okay?"

"I'm fine," she says.

She says it weakly, though. She looks like shit; she looks like she's been tortured for hours. She has blood coming out of her thigh, a bloody nose, and looks like she could fall unconscious at any second, but she is still the most beautiful woman I've ever seen. I need to try negotiating with them, maybe this doesn't have to end the same way as before.

"Let her go," I say, "let all of us go and we will let *you* go. I only came here for her. This doesn't have to end the way it did the last time."

The second killer straightens his back as if he has something to say, trying to look a little more intimidating by standing up a little straighter. He's tall—at least six feet—and the stature reminds me of someone that I can't quite place.

"You're right," the man says, "it's not going to end the same way it did the last time. You're the one who's going to die tonight, Cooper."

I know that voice, I think, *where do I know it from?*

I look over to Dee and it's as if our brains connect for a moment in time. She's thinking the same thing. She has this look on her face that she only gets when she's concentrating or really thinking hard about something. I can just tell that we are thinking the same thing.

"And I'll be the one to do it," the female says, finishing his sentence, "I'll be the one that kills you both, and I'm going to do it slowly."

I hear Riley next to me whisper a very quiet "No" to himself. Does he know her? No, he couldn't, could he?

Is it her? The mystery girl?

I glance at Delilah and she's looking in my direction, but her eyes are fixed on Riley and she gives him a slow nod. Damn, tough break, Riles, but then, with what sounds like the last little bit of energy she has left, Delilah speaks up.

"Watch out Riley," she says.

As the sentence begins to leave Delilah's mouth, Alicia charges at Riley, but with Delilah's warning I'm able to stop her dead in her tracks with a shot to the leg. She falls to the ground and whimpers in pain with blood spewing from the wound.

"Doesn't feel so good, does it?" Delilah says, smirking at me, "stupid bitch."

She rips her mask off to reveal a pretty girl—a very pretty girl. She reminds me of Tatum a little bit, if I'm being honest. She has tears running down her face and she's holding on to the gunshot wound to try to slow the bleeding.

"Alicia, why?" Riley asks.

"Not now—" I start to say, but the man cuts me off.

"You want to know why, Cooper?" he says, "come on, I know you do."

She shoots me a dirty look and I think if she could stand on her own two feet right now, she would come for me.

"Someone start talking," I demand, though I'm really not in a position to make demands, however, I *am* the one holding a gun.

The room fills with silence again, as if they didn't expect to be caught eventually. Are they trying to come up with some sort of story? Alicia keeps glancing at the man as if he holds all the answers. All the while, I'm moving around the room, trying to get closer to Delilah. All I want is to free her, but then I look down at Alicia and now I have a better idea. Quickly, before anyone else in the room can react, I run behind Alicia and wrap my left arm around her neck, lifting her up by it and pressing my gun into her head, dragging her backward and using her as a human shield. The man reacts and is just distracted enough that Riley is able to reach over and grab the knife he was holding, which he points at the man.

"Dad, just tell them!" Alicia screams through sobs as I press the gun harder against the side of her skull.

"Cooper," he says, "it wasn't supposed to end this way. You were never supposed to know who we are."

"Yeah, no shit," I say, sarcasm filling my voice.

"I mean, you were supposed to die, and, don't worry, you will, but she's right. You deserve to know the truth before your life ends."

The man begins to remove his mask. I look back at Riley, who is still pointing the knife at him. As the mask comes off, audible gasps fill the room from myself, Delilah, and Riley. Standing in front of me is Paul, our podcast manager.

"P…Paul?" I say, stunned.

"Knock, knock," he says with a smile, followed by Alicia laughing almost maniacally.

"Who's there?" she says.

I press the gun even harder into her temple to remind her who's in charge here. I look back and forth between Riley and Delilah. I'm too shocked to speak and it looks like the revelation has even woken Delilah up a little up as she sits, still tied to the chair. I drag Alicia backwards and make my way over to Delilah and jerk my head to the right, signaling to Riley to come help me untie her.

"I've got this, untie her," I say.

"Now talk," I say, "this may be your only chance. It's definitely hers."

I grip the gun tighter now, ready to blow her brains all over the walls in this dingy basement. It would be a nice way to round everything out, for her to die just like Tatum did. Who the hell am I? When the thought crosses my mind, I smile slightly. Riley comes over and begins untying Delilah quickly.

"Can you stand?" he says to her.

"Yeah, I think I'm good," she says.

"Start talking, now!" I yell.

"Cooper, come on, you and I both know you're not taking anyone's life tonight. There are three people in this room that are going to die, and Alicia and I aren't a part of that group."

With that one mocking threat, something comes over me and I pull the trigger, gripping the gun tightly to control the kick. Blood and brain matter splatters all over the cinder block wall to my left and I'm left with a lifeless Alicia in my arms. I can feel wetness on my face and realize some of her blood is on me as well. I drop her body to the ground without a care, then focus my aim on Paul.

"No!" he screams, then tries to run to her side.

"Don't fucking move," I say, "tell me now!"

Riley almost has Delilah untied, but jumps back up and points the knife at Paul while I have my sights perfectly set on his chest. He holds up his hands in a sort of fake surrender, then inhales deeply, and exhales.

"Okay," he says. "Here it is: Tom asked me to finish the job that he and Tatum couldn't and I obliged without a question, especially after I saw what your little girlfriend did to Tatum. My little girl, my youngest."

"Tatum was your—" I start, "hold on, *you're* her dad?"

He nods, then says, "Yes, and congratulations, you've taken both of my children from me now."

His eyes are filled with tears, but I can tell he's trying to keep it together, trying to put on a brave face, because now we've given him two reasons to kill all of us. I look over and Riley is now untying the last knot holding Delilah in place. She stands up with a little help from him and comes to my side. Surprisingly, she's not limping too bad, though blood is still seeping from her open wound.

"And you think I care? Tom, Tatum, you, and your stupid little girl," I say, glancing at Alicia's lifeless body, "have taken so much from me. You really think I care about your sob story?"

"Oh, no, I don't, after all, you slept with my Tatum, then killed her. I know you don't care."

"Actually, I did that," says Delilah with a wide smile on her face.

"This isn't over, Cobb," he says, "you're still going to die tonight."

"You're wrong," I say, "you're the one who's going to die."

He starts backing away from us closer to the stairs and we move closer as well to keep him in our sights. If he starts running up the stairs, I'm going to pull the trigger again. This needs to end for good.

"So that's it? Good old-fashioned revenge, huh?" I ask.

He nods.

"That's a little boring for a motive, don't you think? I mean, come on, this is 2023. Come up with something a little more creative than that. It's all a little too Nancy Loomis for me."

Delilah nudges me with her arm. I look over and she smiles at the reference to *Scream 2*. Paul looks confused, but shakes it off and continues backing away.

"This doesn't happen here, Cooper," he says, "I promise you. You know where to find me."

Quickly, he turns and runs up the stairs and I fire off two rounds at him, missing both times. Before I know it, he disappears and I hear the front door open and slam shut. I turn to look at Delilah and holster my gun. I grab her by the waist and run my hand through her hair. She winces a little bit and I pull my hand away when I get to the back of her neck and notice some of her blood on me.

"Are you okay?" I ask.

"I'll be fine, let's get this motherfucker," she says.

"You sure?" I ask, looking for a confirmation.

"I'm going to be there to help you this time," she says, "I will risk my life for you."

Riley clears his throat in a sort of don't-you-have-something-else-to-say way. Delilah looks up at me with her big, beautiful eyes and looks deep into mine, then wraps her arms around my neck.

"I will risk my life *and* his or her life for you," she says, looking down at her stomach.

"Are…are you?" I ask, too stunned to form the words to ask the whole question.

She simply nods and starts to laugh awkwardly. I grab on to her and pull her in for a deep embrace. I take in the scent on her hair. It smells of her shampoo, only it's laced with a little bit of blood. I look over at Riley and he just smiles. I pull back and let go of her.

"Let's go finish this, and Riley, I'm so sorry about that," I say, pointing at Alicia.

"Nah man, fuck her," he says, giving me another smile, "psycho bitch."

The three of us head up the stairs, and when we get to the front door, I pause, and they continue going. Realizing I'm not right behind them, they stop and turn to look.

"What did he mean when he said, you'll know where to find me?" I ask.

Delilah walks back up to me and stares into my eyes, then says, "For a smart guy, you really are dumb sometimes."

I smile at her, then say, "Thanks," rolling my eyes.

"Where did this end last time?" she asks.

"The cemetery," I say, a look of realization flashing across my face.

CHAPTER FIFTY-SIX

COOPER COBB

Without a vehicle, the three of us haul ass on foot trying to make our way to the cemetery. I still can't believe it's Paul and Alicia. I didn't know her, but *him?* The shocking revelation is plaguing my brain, but I have to remain sharp. I need to have my wits about me before we face off against him. Who knows what he may have up his sleeve. He's followed the horror movie rules to a T and became more violent than Tom. He's blown up the house we were in, he's crashed a car into the coffee shop trying to kill us, who knows what else he may try.

The cemetery is only a little over a mile away from Paul's house on Sleepy Hollow Road, but the walk-slash-run there feels like we are running the length of a marathon as we have to keep stopping f0r Delilah to catch up. It could be the anxiety enveloping every fiber of my being right now, it could be the fact that I'm definitely out of shape and could use a little cardio training, but nevertheless, I'm leading the group.

Rounding the corner on Broad Street, I think back to the house and try to remember how many rounds I've shot. Three on the window, one on the handle, and one deep into Alicia's brain. Five left in this magazine. I pat my pocket even though I know my extra is there; the confirmation is nice. So I have fifteen shots left and I will use every single one of them on him if I need to. This needs to end for good.

We are getting to the end of the street when all three of us simultaneously drop our speed and begin to walk as we see the sign for the Milan Cemetery. I unholster my gun and look around, making sure there are no police nearby. The gravel on the road crunches under our feet as we walk the path into the unknown—not knowing exactly what will be waiting for us. We walk slowly and deliberately to keep the noise to a minimum so we can listen for branches snapping or other signs of movement. We don't speak, but the three of us have a sort of conversation with our eyes.

As we walk deeper into the cemetery further away from the houses on Broad Street, it gets darker and the feeling is eerie. There are only a few street lights scattered throughout: a lot of them are flickering and some just have blown out bulbs. I'm squinting my eyes trying to look ahead, but the dark starts to play games with my sight and I keep thinking I'm seeing figures darting between trees.

All of a sudden, a gunshot goes off in the distance and I hear a bullet whiz by my head. I know he's close by and he can see us. I draw my gun, though it probably won't be too effective against a long range weapon. I raise my gun and fire a warning shot, though I'm not sure which direction he is. Out of nowhere, a large, metal object flies between us, which tells me he's close. I strain my eyes again to try to see what it is when I spot a grenade on the ground without a pin.

"Get down, grenade!" I yell urgently.

Just in time for the explosion to go off, the three of us dive in separate directions. As I check on Delilah, I can hear Riley screaming in complete agonizing pain. I jump up and run to his side after I realize she's okay, and I'm met with a terrible sight. Riley is lying on the ground with his left leg missing, blood pouring out of the stump left by the explosion. I quickly grab the button down I'm wearing and rip it off, which sends buttons flying all over, and wrap it around his thigh, tying it tight. I reach over and put my hand on his shoulder as he looks at me with fear in his eyes.

"It's going to be alright, bud," I say, "I promise. We are going to get you out of here."

"Is my leg—" he begins to ask.

"It is. I'm so sorry I dragged you into this. This is all my fault," I say.

"No," he says trying to stifle the pain, "I could have gotten out at any time and I didn't. Don't blame yourself. Just do me one favor."

"What's that?" I ask as another gunshot goes off and the bullet flies past over our heads.

"Kill that motherfucker," he says.

I nod in confirmation. I stand up, run back to Delilah, and look her up and down, grabbing on to her as if I'm trying to hold her in place.

"Are you okay?" I ask again.

"I'm fine," she says, slightly annoyed—almost like she's being inconvenienced.

"Okay, I need you to—" I say, but she cuts me off mid-sentence.

"No," she says with an angry look on her face, "I will *not* leave you this time. I will *not* go get the police. There are houses everywhere, someone is bound to call and report the explosion."

"Okay, but Riley needs medical attention as soon as possible. His leg is missing and he's bleeding pretty badly."

"Watch my back," she says as she crawls away behind a tree.

Not a terrible idea; I get down on my belly and flatten myself as much as I can, but still holding my gun out in front of me. I fire off two more warning shots. I can hear Delilah talking to someone. She must be calling 911. I press the button to release the magazine and drop it to the ground, then reach into my pocket and pull out the other one and slide it into the gun. I'm going to need every round I can get and don't want to get caught having to change out magazines in the middle of a fight.

Delilah crawls back out from around the tree and slides in right next to me. She shouldn't be putting this much pressure on her stomach. I can't believe it, I'm going to be a dad. I don't know what to think, especially at this moment in time. I'm scared, I'm excited, I'm—I really don't know how to feel. I wish she'd have told me sooner.

"The police are about ten minutes out, Coop. If we are going to do this, we need to make it quick," she says.

"Ten minutes is all I need," I say confidently, "you stay back. Please. I will handle Paul. Just stay out of the line of fire."

I have to look at her with a stern face. She will try to follow me. She will try to help me, and I can't have her getting hurt. I'm drowning in my own thoughts when suddenly, I realize that everything around us has grown quiet. Delilah is trying to respond, but I put a finger to my lips and shush her. The look on her face says she's realizing the same thing. That eerie silence has returned. Quickly but quietly, I stand up trying to get a better view of the cemetery in front of me. I don't see anyone running from tree to tree. Maybe he's hiding behind one of them waiting for us to make a move. Delilah follows my lead and begins to stand up as I turn to scan things one more time. Just then, I hear an audible gasp behind me, and I turn quickly to see what's wrong. I'm met with Paul standing with Delilah in his grasp with a knife at her throat.

"The tables have turned, Cobb," he says, "give up now."

CHAPTER FIFTY-SEVEN

DELILAH CARNEY

Please don't kill me. Please don't, I say inside my own head, begging for my life. I try to open my mouth and force the words to come out, but the tears running down my face and my throat tightening up against the sharp, cold blade make it impossible to form words. It can't end like this. I so desperately want to plead for my life, and if I could just form a coherent sentence, maybe I could use the baby as the leverage I need for him to release me.

Just then, I feel a wetness forming between my legs and an intense cramping in my lower abdomen. I try to move my eyes and glance down to maybe get an idea of what's going on but I can't see; all I know is it can't be good. I don't want to think about it, but I think I know what's happening right now. The cramping is so bad, I want to collapse to my knees and wrap my arms around my stomach, but one false move and this blade slides through my throat.

Paul and Cooper are standing in silence with me in the middle. I can feel Paul's hot breath on the back of my neck and I'm staring down the barrel of Cooper's nine-millimeter. I feel like I've already been stabbed in the stomach. This is another level of pain, and the wetness is becoming worse. I see Cooper glance down and also realize what's going on, and his face contorts into an expression that I've never seen before: pure rage.

CHAPTER FIFTY-EIGHT

COOPER COBB

I look down and I can see Delilah's white pants soaked in blood between her legs. She is struggling against Paul's grip and even though I don't want to admit it, I know exactly what's happening to her. It feels like my whole world just got ripped away from me, but at the same time, it's a relief. Now she's my only focus. Now I just have to make sure I save her and maybe we have a chance to make it happen again in the future.

"Paul," I finally say, "it's not her you want. It's me."

"No, I want both of you. You both played a part in taking my Tatum from me."

"I led her to it. I'm fully responsible."

"The way I remember it, they came to you. It was their plan that led you to them. You discovered *nothing*."

I can't argue with him on that point. The only reason I knew it was Tom was because of the random ride I had to give him back to his house when I met him and him messing up by sending the knife with his initials through our window. I think I accidentally confirmed that he's right by my facial expression, because he gives me a smirk like he just defeated me.

"Paul, don't make me do this," I say as I can hear sirens in the distance, "you have two choices right now. Let her go. We will give you a chance to run as long as you let Delilah go."

"I can't. You took everything from me and now, I'm going to take everything from you."

"Then I'm going to end you, just like I ended Alicia." I say.

I can see his expression change immediately when I say her name. I need to take him off guard. I fire a round just past his head and instantly, he drops Delilah to the ground and grabs his ear out of impulse. Delilah runs back to my side. I look at her for a moment as he is incapacitated, she has a small line across her throat with a little bit of blood running out of it, but it's not spewing, so I'm sure she's going to be okay.

Paul stands back up and points the knife at me as he quite literally brought a knife to a gun fight. I can read his body language and see he's about to charge at me, so I quickly fire another round into his leg—the same way I brought Tom to his knees. I fire another round at the hand wielding the knife and as I do, it goes flying through the air and he is now missing three fingers. Two more rounds into his thighs; I need to ensure he won't be getting up again and I want him to suffer.

As if the universe wants this all to feel too familiar, a few drops of rain begin falling from the sky. Faster and faster they drop until we are left in a torrential downpour. Thunder cracks above us and lightning illuminates the night sky. I look up as if to give thanks to whatever higher power exists out there. The storm reminds me that I have the power to end this. I fire another round into Paul's stomach and the sheer force of the close-range shot knocks him down.

I jump on top of him, fully ensuring that he's restrained, and Delilah, following my lead, walks over to him just behind his head, grabs his arms, and pushes them down into the now-muddy grass. The sirens grow louder and closer. I don't have much time to do this. I reach down to the sheath I'd been hiding around my ankle all night and pull out my own Buck 119, my own little souvenir of sorts that I kept as a trophy from killing Tom. I shove it into his face making sure that he can see it.

"You see this?" I ask.

He nods his head in confirmation.

"Do you see those letters? T.L. Tom Langford," I say, "this is the knife I used to kill him, and now, you thought you were him. You tried to be him. You attempted to carry on his legacy. Well, congratulations. Now you're going to die exactly as he did."

He opens his mouth to respond, but before he can, I lift the knife and plunge it deep into his throat, so deep that it goes through the back of his neck and into the dirt beneath him. I turn it clockwise, then counter-clockwise a few times, then rip it back out of his throat. He begins to gurgle as blood runs from the open wound. I force the knife through his chest and pull out as quickly as it went in. I hold the knife up and use my free hand to wipe his blood off of it. Delilah gives me a smirk.

I place it back into the sheath and quickly grab my gun. The police are close and I can see the red and blue lights shining across the darkness. Do I let him bleed out or do I end this right here and right now? If I leave him and the paramedics show up, he has a chance to live and we can't have that. I grab my gun and place it at his temple, pressing in hard. He's still gurgling and trying to form a coherent sentence. I can see true fear in his eyes, but something has taken me over and I don't care. I lean down to send him off with one last thing.

"Say hi to your daughters for me," I say, then pull the trigger. Blood splatters on Delilah's face and mine. She jumps as the bodily fluid hits her right on the lips and immediately lifts her arm to wipe it away. I stand up and look over Paul's lifeless body. Delilah comes to my side and admires my work with me. I place my arm around her as police and paramedics begin to pull up around us.

"I'm sorry," she says as she rests her head on my shoulder, "I'm sorry I couldn't keep our baby safe."

"It's not your fault, babe. Not the right time," I say.

The two of us turn around and walk up to Riley who is already being treated by paramedics. We watch as they put an oxygen mask on his face and start to load him up onto a stretcher.

"You okay there, Riles?" I ask.

"Never better," he responds, giving me a thumbs up.

"Are you two okay?" A paramedic asks us.

We look at one another, considering getting out of here. I'm sure we are going to be stuck in Milan for a little while. I'm going to have to help my mom plan dad's funeral. I sort of just remembered what had happened to him.

"No," I say, "we aren't. She needs to get to a hospital."

Delilah looks at me hoping I wouldn't say that, but I know she needs to get the wound on her thigh and shoulder checked, and much to her dismay, she's going to need to get things checked out by a doctor after the apparent miscarriage. One of the paramedics escorts us to an ambulance and I take the opportunity to take one last look at Paul as police are covering him with a sheet.

CHAPTER FIFTY-NINE

COOPER COBB
TWO DAYS LATER

"The D and C procedure went as well as we could have hoped," said Dr. Roman, in his soothing tone, "we believe we managed to get all of the remaining tissue out and got everything cleaned up for you. I am so sorry for your loss. If you need anything, make sure you reach out to Dr. Jenn. She's the best in her field for dealing with losses as great as these, and she can be a wonderful person if you just need someone to talk to."

Dr. Roman turns on his heels and walks out of the room. I look over and see a tear roll down Delilah's cheek. We were told that she's going to stay here for observation for the next twenty-four hours. She doesn't say a word to me. She just reaches over and grabs the remote and turns on the TV. It's nothing but story after story on every news channel about our heroic end to a tragic story.

Heroes, I think. We aren't heroes; at least, I don't consider us to be by any stretch of the imagination. I don't want anyone to act like we are either. We'd been through this once and I knew we could do it again. Delilah rolls her eyes as she flips through the channels. I know she wants to take her mind off of the things that happened, so I reach over, grab the remote, and turn off the TV. I pull out my phone and queue up something I know will make her happy.

"Which will it be today? One, two, three," I say as I continue to rattle off every installment of *Scream* up to six. She smiles at me.

"Let's do *Scream VI*," she says.

I hand her my phone and a smile curves at the corners of her mouth. It's the first time I've seen her happy in the last couple of days. Actually, it's been a few weeks since this all began, really. I'm watching the movie with her, when I hear a wheelchair rolling into the room. I look up to see Riley sitting in the doorway, smiling at us. I wave him in.

"Hi, Riley," Delilah says, then immediately looks back down at the phone.

"Hey man," I say, "how are you feeling?"

"Been better," he says, but he laughs it off, "the doctor says I'll be up and walking again in about a year with a prosthetic."

I glance at his missing leg, and the same feeling of guilt that I had in the cemetery washes over me. I can't help but feel responsible for this happening to him.

"It's cool," he says, reading my face, "really. Plus, maybe the sob story will help me pick up chicks."

Delilah and I both chuckle.

"Might be best to stay away from the ladies for a little bit, man," I say.

"You're right. The next one might try to kill me too," he replies.

He rolls over to Delilah's other side and begins to watch the movie with us—not really his style, but I know he's doing it to make Delilah feel a bit better, so I'm sure he doesn't mind it right now.

"So what's going on right now?" he asks.

"Samara Weaving is about to pull a horror movie no-no and walk into a dark alley by herself," Delilah says.

"Ah," he says, "not very smart."

"Blondes never are in horror movies."

Suddenly, we hear a ton of commotion going on in the hallway outside of Delilah's room. She hits pause on the movie and the three of us stair at the open doorway. We can hear people screaming outside, and specifically, a woman's voice. I can hear her yelling and it sounds familiar to me. I hear her yell "Tom" out loud so I get up to check things out. I peek outside of the door and what I see terrifies me more than Tom, Tatum, Paul, or Alicia ever did. I can see orderlies scrambling and fighting a woman trying to get her to lay down on a gurney. Then I see them bring in some straps to keep her down. There has to be at least ten people trying to fight her to calm her down.

I turn to walk out of the room and walk up to them, but I'm stopped by a nurse who tells me I need to turn around and go back to our room. I fight to stand on my tiptoes and see what is going on, then I spot her.

"That's my mom," I yell as I push past the nurse and run up to her.

"Mom, mom, what's going on? It's me, Cooper," I say frantically.

Her eyes widen and I can see the fear in them.

"Cooper, no!" she yells at me, then pushes me, making me stumble and fall onto the floor. I'm lifted up by a doctor who then moves me out of the way.

"What's happening to my mom?" I yell at the top of my lungs over the screaming.

The doctor walks back up to me and looks at me with a concerned expression on his face.

"We believe she's suffering from a psychotic break, Cooper," he says.

"A psychotic break?" I ask, echoing his words.

"Yes," he says, "do you know who her medical power of attorney is? We need someone in their right mind to make some decisions that she can't currently make."

I'd not thought about it. With my dad gone, I guess I'm the only one that can make those decisions.

"I…I guess it's me," I say, "my dad died two days ago and my so-called brother died a few months ago. I'm all she has."

"Do we have your permission to give her a sedative then?" he asks.

"Absolutely, do what you have to do," I say.

They struggle to get her down, but they finally do and strap her to the gurney. I watch a nurse walk over to her with a syringe and quickly plunge it into her backside, injecting the medicine inside. Almost instantly, her body relaxes and she stops fighting with everyone. Her eyes close and she goes to sleep. There's nothing I can do but simply walk away and go back to our room. I walk back in, sit down, and I can feel Delilah and Riley staring at me.

"Is everything okay?" Riley asks.

I don't respond. I dissociate almost completely. I can feel my heart rate speeding up and dizziness taking over my head. I feel like I'm going to be sick and my hands begin to shake uncontrollably. It feels like my head is physically spinning around on my neck like a top. Blackness fills the edges of my field of vision, then slowly creeps in until I'm left in complete darkness. I feel my body go limp and fall to the ground. I can hear Delilah screaming, but it sounds like I'm underwater until everything fades away and I'm left with nothing.

MORE TITLES BY STEVEN T. THOMAS

Who's There? (Knock Knock Series Book 2)
Guess Who (Knock Knock Series Book 3)

ABOUT THE AUTHOR

Steven T. Thomas is an Independent Author from Dryden, MI. He enjoys watching Horror Movies and listening to Metal music. When he isn't working or writing, he is busy spending time with his wife and two children.